TAGGED STEEL

MJ FIELDS

mj fields

Real, Raw, Romance

COPYRIGHT

1st Edition

Published by Blue Valley Publishing LLC

Cover Design by Jersey Girl Design

Edits by C&D Editing

Proofed by Wicked Proofing

Cover model Andrew England

SYNOPSIS

Living by my father's rules has never been easy.

Who does he think he is anyway? Jase Steel has broken every rule he tries to make me live by.

The Four Ds:

~~No Dating~~ (Thanks to Carly and Momma Joe, that was nixed at sixteen.)

~~No Drinking~~ (Shots of Jack at prom.)

~~No Drugs~~ (College frat party and a bear-shaped bong named Smokey.)

The last one though, that last D, ruined my virgin skin, my relationship with my father, and changed my whole life.

~~No Decorating~~

I should have listened to him ... but I didn't.

Tag—I'm it.

DEDICATION

CC
In sixth grade, foot to junk, loyalty was birthed. You taught me the true meaning. We became family by choice.
This series was born of that bond.
I miss you so fucking much.
Until we meet again you are now and forever... steel.

Forever Steel,
ME

TO THE READER

Six years ago on July 13th Jase was released.

What better day to release Bella's story.

I hope you enjoy.

Forever Steel,

MJ

PART ONE

BELLA

Prequel

ONE
BEING THE DAUGHTER OF JASE STEEL

Sunday dinner is a Steel family tradition. We rotate between Momma Joe and Thomas's, Cyrus and Tara's, Zandor and Bekkah's, Xavier and Taelyn's, and our house. Today, it's at our place.

Eleven of us are at the regular dining room table, with the eight youngest Steels seated at the kids' table. Salad and garlic knots have been served, and lasagna and roasted vegetables are being plated and passed around.

Like Garfield, lasagna is my father's favorite, so I decide this is the absolute best time, and safest place, to tell my father, at sixteen, that Chad Wentworth asked me to a movie the following Friday night. My very first date.

The normally, noisy room falls silent, even the kids' table decides to follow suit, and that didn't even happen when Momma Joe said the blessing.

Uncle Cyrus, the oldest of the four, is the first to speak. "You shoot the first one, word will spread."

His wife, my aunt Tara, covers her face and shakes her head.

"That's enough, Cyrus," Momma Joe scolds him.

"Tell him, whatever he does to our Little Bell, Zandor will do to him." Xavier chuckles and so does his wife Taelyn.

I look at Uncle Zandor as he smirks, shrugs, looks at his wife Bekkah, and then asks, "You okay with that?"

"None of y'all are right," she replies, sitting back and taking a healthy drink of her wine.

When I look back to Dad, I realize that his eyes haven't left me and there is no expression to be read in them ... at all.

Then he simply states, "No."

I hear a large *thud*, then he whips his head left. "What the hell, Carly?"

"She's sixteen, for God's sake," she whispers like no one will hear her.

We all do.

They have a stare off until he finally looks over at me. "Let's talk about God, shall we?"

"Really?" I roll my eyes.

"Jase," Momma Joe snips quietly.

"With all due respect, Momma, you raised four amazing men, but girls, well, they're nothing like boys."

"You don't say?" Momma Joe slowly raises an eyebrow.

"I know you've helped us the whole way, but this is my little girl."

"She's sixteen," Momma Joe and Carly say at the same time.

I figuratively raise a victorious fist in the air, and then I just sit back and listen to them bicker.

Out of the corner of my eye, I notice my sister Kiki and my cousin Truth watching it all go down, eyes darting back and forth like they're watching a tennis match. When Kiki looks at me, she smirks, and I give her a wink.

It's a win.

* * *

IT'S THURSDAY OR, as I am secretly deeming it, first date eve.

After Kiki's piano lesson, Carly, Kiki, and I got haircuts. When we started walking out of the salon, Momma Joe was walking in.

"Three of my favorite girls." She hugs us all. "Would you care to join me for mani/pedis?"

"Heck yes!" Kiki squeals. "Perfect idea! Tomorrow's date night, Momma Joe."

The wink shared between my seven-year-old sister and my grandmother makes it obvious this was planned, even before we are greeted by the staff and brought back to the four pedicure chairs already waiting for us

"I think she's more excited about your date than you, if not even more so," Momma Joe says with a laugh as we sit.

"Don't let her fool you," Carly whispers. "She has an ulterior motive. She's just hoping you break him in so it's not as difficult when it's her turn."

Kiki smiles. "I already have a boyfriend."

"You do, do you?" Momma Joe asks.

She nods. "He just doesn't know it yet."

"Dad doesn't or the boy doesn't?" I ask my bright-eyed little sister.

"Neither!" She laughs hysterically at herself.

After we're finished, Carly asks Momma Joe to come over for dinner.

"I would love to," Momma Joe replies.

The look exchanged between them also tells me that this was planned.

* * *

WHEN WE PULL up the driveway, Dad is filling the doorway, my brother Max beside him. As Momma Joe rolls up behind us, he narrows his eyes, and Carly smirks as she waves.

All week, he's been extra. Extra edgy, extra stress-y, extra ... just extra.

Carly has been keeping me close, and when they don't think I'm in earshot, she's keeping him in check, telling him, "I see what you're doing." Or, "You better check yourself, Steel, or you'll be on the couch." Or, "She's sixteen, Jase, and she's a hell of a lot more street smart than I ever was. She'll be fine. It's him you should feel bad for."

When we walk up the front steps, he looks at me. "Got a minute, Bella?"

"She's already promised to help me get dinner on the table." Carly smirks as she pushes up on her tiptoes and gives him a loud peck on the cheek.

"Carly," he grumbles as Kiki leaps at him.

"Catch me, Daddy!"

Momma Joe and Carly keep Dad busy the entire night; Kiki even seems to be in on it.

By the time he has read to Max, and Kiki has made him listen to her newest song, in which she has also choreographed—on the fly, I'm sure—I have showered and shut myself in my room.

Lying in bed, unable to sleep, looking at the time on my phone as I switch between scrolling through Instagram and watching Snapchat stories, I hear a light knock on my door before it is opened.

Dad.

He walks in. "Scooch." He sits on the edge of my bed

and waits for me to move over before lying on top of my duvet.

"Not gonna say I'm always rational."

I stifle a laugh.

He raises an eyebrow then continues, "Got you back less than ten years ago, Little Bell. So, to me, you're ten, not sixteen, making this extremely hard."

I want to point out that is a messed-up way of thinking, a piss poor excuse for treating me like I'm Kiki's age, but I also don't want to get grounded.

He looks at me, expecting me to say just that, but I know better.

"I love you, Bella."

"I love you, Dad."

"I know you're smart, but I also know the mind of a teenage boy, because I was one. I have a few things I need you to hear, Bella, *really* hear about dating."

I roll to my side and look at him.

He takes a deep breath then exhales slowly. "They earn every fucking thing you give them, starting with a yes to him asking for a date. Did he earn it?"

"I think he did. Before I even asked you. I told him he'd have to pull into my driveway, get out, and meet my family before I'd be allowed to leave the premises."

He fights to hold back a smile, then it's gone. "You don't put yourself in a situation you don't feel comfortable being in. No means no."

"He hasn't even sent me a message that is suggestive at all."

His eyes widen, and his jaw tenses before he says, "You said he; have others?"

"I'm sixteen. Sexting is—"

"Not dating. Any little fuck sends you sexual messages—"

"They get blocked."

"They?" His voice is higher than I've ever heard.

"I'm going to a movie, Dad. We're meeting friends—"

"I can drop you off at a movie, where you can—"

"Dad," I groan exaggeratedly. "You told me when I got my license that I could ride in a car with my friends. I haven't yet."

"Never said boyfriends," he grumbles.

"Never said he was my boyfriend, Dad. It's a first date."

He stares at me; I stare back. Then he nods.

"What do you really want to say?" I ask.

"He doesn't deserve you."

"He's a friend, who asked me on a date, not for a freaking—"

"Don't you dare," he warns.

"Then trust me, Dad. Trust. Me. He's not the one you should be afraid of."

"What the fuck is that supposed to mean?"

"It means he's the first one to ask, not the 'first' one." I air quote *first*. "I'm not going to sleep with the first boy I date, get knocked up, and—"

"That's not cool, Bella."

"Then tell me what you want to tell me, Dad."

"He doesn't deserve you," he states matter-of-factly, again.

"How will I know if anyone deserves me, Dad? I haven't even been kissed."

He doesn't even fight to hide his smile this time. He beams.

I flop back on my pillow. "Oh my God, can I just go to sleep?"

"When you even think he's possibly the boy who deserves your first kiss, Bella, you make damn sure he deserves you. Which means you know him. You know he treats his momma right, because that's the way he'll treat you. You remember you can do anything he can, and if he makes you feel like that's not the case, he's out. You remember to still dress like you and don't change for him. No over-the-top makeup shit, Little Bell. Never let him think for you. Don't get your head stuck up your ass, because the right guy for you will love that you're intelligent and can think for yourself. And remember, you never have to do anything to make someone love you. The right person will cross the fucking desert in tin foil just to open a door for you."

He pushes his arm under my head and pulls me into a hug. "Compare every single boy you ever meet to the man I was when you came back into my life. Nobody will love you like I do. If he even comes close, I will shake his hand and give him my blessing."

TWO
DATE NIGHT

I'm done getting ready for my date long before Chad is expected to pick me up so that I could be out the door ASAP, giving little time for Dad to embarrass me.

When Chad, the son of two doctors, shows up in his BMW to take me to a movie, Dad beats me to the door.

"Come on in, Chad." His smile is big, bright, and welcoming.

I feel it's safe to allow such a thing for two reasons. One, it's a first and he doesn't seem all that "Jase Steel" over it. And two, I overheard Carly threatening him with a week on the couch if he was, in her words, an asshole.

I start to feel good about this meet and greet ... until Chad smiles back, walks in, and I see Dad narrow his eyes as he glares at the back of his head.

Then Dad offers him a beer, to which Chad thankfully declines, saying, "I'm sorry, sir, but I'm not of legal age, nor would I put your daughter in harm's way by drinking even a sip of alcohol before driving her in my vehicle."

Nice, I think ... until I see Dad looking at him with his eyes and jaw set.

"Chad"—the way Dad says his name is rather obnoxious —"you've never had a drink?"

"Yes, sir, with my parents on Christmas, I had some spiked eggnog, and it was disgusting." He laughs, and Dad narrows his eyes.

"Hey, Chad, I'm Katherine Steel, Little Bell's sister."

Little Bell? Ugh, seriously?

I turn and see her reaching out her hand to shake his and notice the tee-shirt she's wearing.

On top, it says, "*Heads-up, Boys.*" Below it is a picture of my father, shirtless, inked, and jacked. Below that, it says, "*This is my father.*"

I notice Chad's eyes widen, and then he smiles and shakes Kiki's hand. "Pleasure to meet you."

Max runs into the room in one of Kiki's tutus ... and nothing else on.

I glare at Dad, and he holds his hands up as if to say, *wasn't me.*

When Carly walks into the kitchen, her smile falls as she looks at Kiki then at Dad. "Really?"

He grins. "Hey, Carly, can I get you a drink?"

She sighs. "Make it a double." Then she looks at Chad. "Hi there, I've heard a lot about you."

And now, I want to crawl under the table.

He smiles. "All good, I hope."

As if things couldn't possibly get any worse, I hear Uncle Cyrus ask, "Anybody home?"

I shoot Dad a look, and he bites back a smile.

"Well, we should get going," I say, nodding toward the door. "Don't want to be late."

Chad looks back at my parents. "Nice meeting you." When he turns around, he looks up as Uncle Cyrus walks basically into him. Chad looks stunned.

I shoot Cyrus the same look I just shot my dad, thinking if the other two show up, I'm going to be out of ammunition really quick.

"Chad, this is my uncle Cyrus." I literally push Cyrus aside with my hip, and he chuckles. "And we're going to be late."

"Nice, me-me-meeting you." Chad hurries past the intense glare Cyrus appears to be giving him, but it's honestly his natural expression.

We're at the threshold, and I think we're clear, when I hear Cyrus say, "Hey, Chad." Saying *Chad* in the same tone my father used.

We both turn as he tosses something to him.

Chad catches whatever was thrown, looks at it, and then closes his hand around it.

Cyrus smiles menacingly. "Those come much faster after ten o'clock, you feel me?"

"Yes, sir." Chad then hurries past me and toward his car.

"What the hell was that?" I snap at my uncle.

He shrugs. "It was an anti-condom."

"What's an ant condo?" Max asks from behind him.

"What did he just say?" Carly asks.

"It's a place little insects crawl into." Cyrus smirks as he picks Max up. "Dude, what the hell are you wearing?"

"It's a three-three."

I walk out and don't look back.

When I get in the vehicle, I look at Chad. "I'm sorry for whatever just happened."

"Is this"—he pauses, his face pinches up—"normal?"

I answer honestly, "Nothing about my family is normal. What did he throw at you?"

He nods to the cup holders in the console. "A bullet."

"Oh, my freaking God," I groan.

Before even leaving the driveway, I already know Chad won't be anything more than a friend. *Why*, you ask?

First, he ran out of my house like he was going to piss himself. Then he didn't even open the door for me. The kicker was the pinched face. *That* pissed me off.

My family may not be "normal," but they're pretty amazing. I would never be with someone who didn't at least find humor in them. And if I am being honest with myself, I only said yes to this date in order to open doors to dating, and if Chad didn't run his mouth about Kiki's shirt, Max's tutu, or Cyrus's bullet, I should have been fine.

But he did.

However, it didn't detour others from asking. In fact, I had several boys ask me out. Some I even accepted their invitations.

Every time I had a date, which wasn't often, Dad insisted on meeting them before said date. Nine times out of ten, my uncles would be there when said date showed up. And ten times out of ten, I realized they just weren't, as Dad said, worthy.

I want a man who looks at me the way my father and uncles look at their wives. I want a man who doesn't try to change me. I want a man who doesn't cower at any of the warnings my father gives.

I held my V-card all the way through high school, and guess what? It doesn't bother me one fucking bit.

THREE
EIGHTEEN TO LIFE

When I turned eighteen, Dad told me, "You're still not an adult."

I countered with, "I'm eighteen, so the law says otherwise."

He pointed up at the ceiling. "I make the laws in this house. You're still under my roof, the rules still apply."

The rules, you ask.

Let me introduce you to the four Ds.

"No drinking." He scowled.

"So I'll die of dehydration in what, a few days?"

"Don't be a wiseass. I mean of the alcoholic persuasion."

"It's illegal, so we're good."

He arched an eyebrow. "No drugs."

"Same response from the previous. Illegal."

"No decorating your body. Meaning, no tattoos or piercings, other than your ears."

Hypocrite much? I say yes.

"No serious dating."

By serious, he means sex.

"V-card's still intact, Dad. You can thank yourself for that."

"Let's be real here; none of those little pissants from the past even deserved so much as a kiss, Little Bell. So, as much as I'd like to take credit, that was all you making smart choices."

Again, *hypocrite*, but he's not wrong. I did make smart choices.

I don't hate his rules, even though he was having sex with my mom long before he graduated from high school. I have heard stories that he drank when he was going through the loss of her, and me. And *hello*, tattoos and piercings? He was a freaking tattoo artist, and from what I've overheard, he's got piercings in places I wouldn't allow a needle to go near, let alone impale me.

Also, *gross!*

He met Carly when she wasn't even out of college, so again, he's being a hypocrite. But also, he's being protective and, even though I'm supposed to rebel, I just feel it's not my time yet.

I think back on all the horrible things my maternal grandfather said about him and about the stories my maternal grandmother told me in secret, the contradictions. Through those stories and pictures she shared with me when we met, I was able to see him for the man he really is. Through the stories he has shared with me over the years, I understood him not wanting me to go through what he and our family endured. I understood his hypocrisy came from a good place, a place of care and concern.

When I went to college, Dad told me he was *still* paying for the roof over my head, so his rules still applied, and he added more.

No going anywhere alone.

No going anywhere after dark.

No boys in my dorm.

No parties where some shitbag could slip a pill in my Kool-Aid, since I wasn't allowed to drink.

And no sex *ever*.

I broke a few and got caught. Then I realized he was tracking my phone. I was livid, so I went to the source of all things Steel—Momma Joe—to find out how to negotiate with a terrorist—him.

She laughed and told me that he just didn't want me to take the path he had.

I might have known that I was tugging on heartstrings when I reminded her of where his path led—to me. Then I added a smile and the words, "Look at him now. Look at *us* now. Forever Steel."

"Bella, he's tracking your cell phone because he worries about you." She sighed. "As a parent, we don't want our children to struggle like we did. His overprotective ways are out of love."

"But ..." I began.

She held up her hand, stopping me. "However"—she winked—"as long as someone knows you're okay, I see no reason that you can't let your hair down every once and awhile."

"S*o* ..."—I tried to hold back my victory smile—"I can just leave my phone in the dorms when I decide to ... let my *hair down*?"

"Absolutely not." She laughed. "That's *folle*."

Momma Joe gave me a new escape system, via a new phone and a system where I checked in with her.

In that very short amount of time, between l*et your hair down* and Momma Joe slapping me with Italian—*folle* meaning insane—I went to a hundred parties, walked in the dark ... alone, went out past eleven at night ... on a school night, had a boyfriend who wasn't a complete douche, had sex without the threat of seeing my father around every corner, in every shadow, and no, I didn't feel threatened by my dad in the least, but everyone else in a ten-block radius sure as hell did. He made damn sure of it.

PART TWO

STEEL

MEN OF STEEL

Present Day

FOUR
TAG TIME

TAGS

Standing inside Body Art, I see four girls outside of my buddy Sisco's studio.

He smirks. "They're fucked up."

"The little blonde isn't. She looks terrified."

He chuckles. "She looks like that cartoon character."

I nod. "Alice from Alice in Wonderland."

"Wonderland would pass out quicker than the little badass."

"Purple hair, dark skin?" I ask then take a sip of my coffee. "I think you're wrong."

"If I'm wrong, you get dibs on which one you ink. And the cash, too. I'm right, you get Wonderland and I get the cash."

I reach out to shake his hand. "You're on."

Two seconds later, purple hair throws up and we laugh.

When the other one, the one with the long, thick, brown hair and perfect curves, turns and I see her face, my heart skips a beat, maybe two. She's fucking gorgeous.

Living art.

Sparkling blue eyes, lightly tanned skin.

Tag, I think. "She's it."

He chuckles as he looks at the one I'm pointing at. "Beverly?"

"Fuck that." I laugh.

"You have a type, Tags—Beverly Hills."

"I don't have a type. I'm perpetually single. And Sisco, those eyes, they're not Beverly Hills; they're too deep for that."

Only half of it's a lie. I do go for women who are socioeconomically out of my league. And not because I think I want to be like them. I don't. Quite the opposite. I want them to realize money isn't shit. That they just want all the crap that I find nonessential. Shit I'll never have. I just happen to have a thing for fucking shit up for the man she's under while still thinking about me. Men who need arm candy and the newest Porsche in their garage, next to last year's discarded model.

She's not Beverly Hills. She's fucking perfect.

I turn to walk behind the frosted glass to prep as Sisco yells back, "They're getting in a cab. Guess we both lose."

For some reason, I don't stop the setup.

A few minutes later I hear Sisco, "We're closing up."

"But I—" *Sexy voice.*

"We open tomorrow at eleven," he cuts her off.

"Sisco, I can take this one."

"You got cash?" he asks her.

"I do." She sounds excited.

Virgin, I think.

"She's all yours," he calls back to me.

"Perfect." I begin walking out front.

"Lock up and come meet me at the gym when you're done."

"Will do."

When I see her, she looks at me like I did her. Fortunate for me, I get to see it.

"You ready?"

She doesn't reply.

"How deep you want it?"

Her jaw drops, and I eat it up. Double inuendo, and she got it.

I step to her and lift her chin to close her gaping mouth. Her skin feels like silk.

"I like the path your thoughts are traveling on, sweets, but I'm asking about the work you're here to get. You want just the tip of my creativity or do you want me to go all-in?" I step back just a fraction, and her jaw drops again. This time, I'm close enough to help her out again, and luckily for me, she allows it ... again. Then I step back farther, because the way her blue pools are shimmering, and her face flushes, if I don't, shit's going down right here on the floor.

"I have my artwork." She looks down at a large leather bag and begins pulling out what I can guess is a printout of something that she found on the internet—a flower, a lady-bug, something every girl wants. But this one, well, I clearly want to give it to her ... deeper.

"Not how I work." I walk past her and out the door, putting space between us.

"Wait. What?" She gasps, and I know she's following me.

I reach in my pocket and pull out a smoke. Then I lean back against the brick and take a long drag as I watch her watching me. I exhale slowly while breathing it back through my nose.

She's watching me intently, eyes still liquid, face still flush.

"Your concept, my art."

She holds up her paper. "So, you don't want my work?"

I look away, not wanting to see it. I get a sort of high when a client looks at my work on them for the first time, the emotions it produces when I nail their idea, and I always nail it. "Nope."

"You being serious?"

"Dead serious." I look back at her as she rakes her lip between her teeth. "And you keep looking at me like that, and I'm gonna give you what you want then tag you with my art."

"Like what?" She feigns innocent when I can already tell better.

"Like you've never had a man like me between your legs and you desperately want it to happen."

"I'm only looking at you like that because you're looking at *me* like that."

Fuuuuck, I think as she rolls her eyes slightly and mumbles something under her breath.

"You're a beautiful young woman; of course I'd like to fuck you. You just need to decide what comes first."

"Meaning?"

"You want me to decorate you or make you messy first?"

"How about you do your best, and if I like what you do, I'll—"

"Say it, sweets," I cut her off because, if she says what I know she's thinking, I'm going to get arrested when I lay her out on the street. "I dare you."

I flick my smoke into the gutter, reach over, and then open the door, cutting her off again, "Ladies first."

She nods once, her eyes still dancing between mine, then turns and walks in.

I shut the door behind me and lock it. When I turn

around to see if maybe that freaked her out a little, I see her walking behind the frosted glass.

Apparently not.

"Give me a minute. I'll be right with you," I say before walking into the bathroom to wash my hands and brush my teeth so I don't smell like smoke.

When I come out, she's standing by the tray of sterile equipment in a tee-shirt and white, lacey boy shorts. Her back stiffens, but she doesn't turn around.

"I'm aware you don't want to see my drawing, but—"

"More interested in the concept." *And your ass,* I think as I stare at its perfection.

She turns around, looking down at her work, hair covering her face. "It's to honor the women who made me who I am."

"Living or deceased?" I ask as I grab a sketchpad.

"Both," she says, looking up at me.

"Tell me about—"

"Are you really going to just ignore what was said out there?"

I lean against the counter and cross my arms.

"I mean, that was pretty ... you know." She shrugs.

"Honest?"

She looks up, trying not to smile as she shakes her head.

"Crude?"

"I thought so, too. I mean, the way you were eyeballing me made me a little uncomfortable. Made me feel like a piece of meat."

She laughs. "What?"

"I accept your apology. Now—"

"You're an ass." She shakes her head.

"Oh, sweets, that's just the tip"—I pause—"of the proverbial iceberg that is me."

She blushes while shaking her head again. "You really can't talk to people like that in today's political climate."

"I didn't talk to *people*. I talked to you, and your thoughts were screaming at me."

"So, this isn't like a normal thing for you?" After she asks the question, she looks like she regrets it.

I take a step toward her and hold out my hand. She hesitates.

"You walked into this studio with me, walked back here, lost your little sweater, dropped your skirt after all those words out there were exchanged, and now you hesitate? Stop it." I push my hand out farther, and she takes it. Then I turn her toward the mirror and stand behind her.

"Truth." I begin, and she looks up at my reflection, a little shaken, "I don't work here. It's my buddy's studio. In two days, I'm going away from anywhere between six to nine months." Her eyes widen, and I laugh.

"Not jail." *Not this time,* I think to myself. "Where I'm going, I, for damn sure, won't run into anyone who looks like you, who looks at me like you do, and I'm pretty sure they won't taste like you're going to."

She bites her lower lip.

"So, there's my excuse. Now, sweets, what's yours?"

"Huh?" She blinks her eyes that have been glued to the reflection of my mouth since I mentioned tasting her.

"I told you my story; now tag, you're it."

"Graduating college tomorrow. Then I'm going home to pack for a wedding."

The way she says *home* concerns me. "Is home a bad place?"

She shakes her head. "I just have a very overprotective father."

"If you were mine, I can't say if I'd have let you out of my sight."

We stare at each other for a few moments. Then she tilts her head back and licks her lips. I move closer and stop just before my lips touch hers.

"Why?" she whispers.

"Because, when you look at a man like me, you should be crossing the damn street to safety on the other side."

"You put a group of suits on one side of the street and a group of men who look like you on the other, I'm going toward you. Now kiss me or ink me."

I pull back slightly. "Give me the concept."

"You're kidding me, right?" she whispers.

Stepping back, I nod. "I'm going to decorate you first."

She sighs. "I may change my mind, you know."

My lips twitch upward. "Uh-huh."

"It's not like this is normal for me."

"It's also not like you're completely sober, sweets. By the time I'm done, you will be." I sit on my chair and put my feet up on the table. "Tell me the concept."

"The story behind it?" she asks, sitting on the table.

"Absolutely not." I smirk. "That taints the vision."

"Four women have given me great inspiration through beauty, wisdom, strength, and love."

I begin to sketch. "I don't love flowers, per say, but daisies look like they're full of life and are highly detailed."

"Also my favorite," she says.

"Interesting." I sit forward and begin drawing. "I don't want details, but some of the women are no longer here, so one flower fully in bloom, another open but not completely, and another just opening. A lifespan of sorts yet never gone."

She leans over and watches me draw. Normally, I hate that. With her, I like it.

Once the flowers are sketched out, I write the words *She is Beauty* on the upper left, beside the flower not yet fully opened. To the right of the flowers and a little lower, I write *She is Wisdom.* To the left and lower, *She is Strength.* To the right, *She is Love.*

"That's perfect."

I nod and continue. To the left, aligned with *Beauty*, I write, *She is… Me*

After looking it over and adding some detail, I give the sketch a satisfactory nod and look up.

Lust is now replaced by emotion in her eyes.

"*She is me*," she whispers, looks up, and smiles softly. "I love it." Her smile widens. "I absolutely love it."

"I'm glad, because this is what you're getting." I toss the book on the floor then look her over. "Just not sure where yet. Turn for me."

She slides off the table as I pull my feet down. I push my chair back and look over her rocking body.

"Not the shoulder or neck."

She looks over her shoulder at me. "Somewhere private?"

I reach forward and take her hips. "Bend."

"Not a tramp stamp either."

I nod. "Definitely not."

I turn her body slightly to the side. "Not here. Turn again."

She does.

I let go of her then hold my hands out in frame formation and look through it. Middle lower back. I take the back of my fingertips and run them over the area. "Here."

"That big?"

"Would you rather have an eight-by-ten or a wallet-sized photo hanging on your wall?"

She looks down. "More a five-by-seven, don't you think?"

I lean back and cross my arms. "Might not be the best person to ask that." I wave my hand in front of me. "I like my art visible."

"I'd like mine private."

"Seven by nine?" I push.

She smiles and shrugs.

"So, basically, you'll show it off at the beach and when you're ..." I stop when she turns and looks down my body. "You okay?"

"I'd like some water."

"Thirsty?"

She nods and looks back up into my eyes.

Welcome back, lust. I groan to myself.

I wink then turn and walk out of the room. I know her eyes are still on me.

* * *

SHE'S LYING on her belly and squirming so much that I'm stopping every couple of minutes. It's all good, though; the view is amazing. She's a perfect canvas. Her ass is in my face so when I'm not working on her, I'm sizing her up. It's round, hard, flawless skin, and each cheek is a perfect handful.

"You want me to change things up? Leave out some detail?"

"Fuck no," she groans. "I'd never come back."

I chuckle, almost done. "Good, because I wouldn't have anyway."

"I can't believe people do this all the time."

"It can be addicting."

"Says who?" She cringes when I turn my machine back on.

"Millions of people."

"I'm aware. But at this moment ..." She pauses when I begin again. "Fuck me."

"We'll never get to that if you don't lie still."

She looks back at me, smiling and blushing. "You better be good at what you do."

"Sweets"—I wink—"I don't do anything half-assed."

She props herself up on her elbows and arches her back so I have to stop.

I place my palm between her shoulder blades. "Almost there."

"That's what you said like ..." She pauses to think.

I fill in the blank, "Two minutes ago."

"I better get a sticker or a sucker when this is over. A treat." She lies down and looks back at me. "Finish me off."

"I plan on it."

She lowers her head so her dark chocolate tresses fall in her face, but I see her smirk, her nose crinkling, and her nibbling on her lower lip.

She is ... me. That's all I have to ink to finish the art.

"Three words, and then we'll see what you've got."

FIVE
THE LAST D
BELLA

Three and a half hours ago, I stood outside of Body Art NYC with my three roommates on the eve of our graduation.

"We're really going to do this?" Alice, who looks like a human version of Alice in Wonderland asked, giving them time to contemplate what they had less time to ponder than me. I'd already decided.

I'd be getting my first and maybe last tattoo.

"Fuck yes, we are," Lily said through a hiccup.

We had just left a private rooftop party hosted by a fellow graduate, promising to return after checking the last D off my list of Dad's don'ts.

Victoria looked at me. "If we aren't going in, then we need to get back to The Empire. I have a very handsome young man waiting to buy me a drink."

"Gordon's roommate." Alice nodded then shook her head like she was trying to understand why Victoria would even consider sleeping with her ex-boyfriend's roommate.

She shrugged. "He's hot."

Lily grinned. "He's hung, too."

"Aw, fuck no!" Victoria cried out. "You did not—"

Lily held up a finger. "Just once."

"You've got to be bloody kidding me?" Victoria palmed her face then looked at me. "I need to get back."

"I'll go with you," Alice offered all too easily then looked at me. "If you don't mind?"

Lily took that opportunity to run to the nearest trash can and throw up.

"I don't mind as long as you take her, too."

"But—"

I cut Alice off, "I need to do this."

"I'll stay with you," Lily offered, wiping her face with the back of her hand.

"You'll get us kicked out. Go."

"No woman is left behind!" Lily threw a fist in the air then stumbled.

"I'll take an Uber. Just go."

As soon as they were off, I turned to walk into the building when the neon light turned off.

"You've got to be fucking kidding me." I pushed the door open anyway.

"We're closing up," a man probably my father's age said.

"But I—"

"We open tomorrow at eleven." He smiled.

"Sisco," I heard a man with a deep voice say, "I can take this one."

The man, whose name was Sisco, lips slowly turn up in the corners, and then he looked back at me. "You got cash?"

"I do." I smiled, excited that I was finally, at twenty-three years old, going to get my first and maybe last tattoo.

He looked back toward the room behind the partition. "She's all yours."

"Perfect," he said.

"Lock up and come meet me at the gym when you're done."

"Will do."

When Sisco walked past me, I saw a man walk around the frosted glass partition and—

"You ready?"

OhmyGod, I thought as I looked him over. Six foot plus of bulging muscles covered in more ink than I think I'd ever seen on one person. All black, too, my favorite. And as amazing as *all* that was, the man's face was chiseled perfection, with soul-capturing, light brown, no hazel eyes, that seemed to be getting darker by the minute. Medium-sized diamond studs in his ears, and a small nose ring is in his left nostril.

He looked me up and down. "How deep you want it?"

My jaw dropped, and he pursed his lips. Then he moved them from left to right and back again, trying not to smile, but those stunning eyes were doing just that as he reached out a finger and lifted my chin.

My mouth went dry, my heart was racing, and no words came out. I knew immediately that I was in way over my head but, my God, what a way to end my college career.

AND NOW, I'm lying nearly bare-assed in an unfamiliar yet very familiar environment, trying my best not to drool over the most amazing piece of male perfection that I have ever seen while he permanently marks me.

So hot.

The pain is nearly unbearable, if not for the way he seems to know when I've had enough, or the way he makes small talk with double entendres.

Sexy as hell double entendres.

When he reaches across the space to pull a wheeled silver tray with the salve and dressing for my tattoo—*my tattoo!*—I can't help grinning.

I look over my shoulder at him to see his eyes crinkle in a small smile as he begins to tell me about aftercare.

"You'll need to keep this covered ..."

The rest of his words fall on deaf ears as I watch him look over my body like he wants to undress the rest as he dresses the art. When he's finished, he stands.

I watch him, unmoving, as he kicks the wheeled stool aside and takes the one step it takes him to get to the end of the table. Then he grips my hips and pulls me toward him slowly. Looking back at him, I know my own eyes mirror his —heat to heat, lust to lust.

When my feet hit the floor, he kicks them to the sides, spreading my legs wider. "Never fucked in a studio." His eyes leave mine as he scans my body. "You want it right here, right now?"

I raise an eyebrow and only half-joke, "Was the tattoo foreplay or do you have more in you than that?"

His lips quirk upward. "My impulse control is shit, sweets. Got me in trouble back in the day. So, you want my tongue between your thighs, I suggest you get naked."

"What?" I gasp.

"Naked is when there is nothing between my skin and yours." He narrows his eyes then smirks when he realizes what his words may have led me to believe. He waves his hand up and down his body then points to his face. "Really?"

I stand and pull my tee-shirt over my head, rolling my eyes at myself. "Right."

His eyes are no longer twinkling mischief as he pulls his

white V-neck over his head with one hand. They are nearly black and completely liquid ... just like my panties.

"Your tits are ..." He swipes his tongue over his full lips as he looks at me like I've seen ...

Oh, hell no, I scold myself. *It's bad enough you're fucking in a tattoo shop; there is no room for Jase or Jesus up in this place.*

"Lose the panties, sweets," he says, snapping me out of my disgusting thought process.

"Lose the pants, gorgeous," I counter as I slip my thumbs under my waistband.

He cocks his head to the side and looks almost ... shocked.

"You are—"

He narrows his eyes as he pulls a condom out of his pocket, holds it to his beautiful mouth, and says, "Drop 'em."

As he tears open the foiled packet with his teeth, I narrow my eyes. "You show me yours, I'll show you—" I gasp when he drops his pants. "You're—"

"You lick it, it's yours."

My mouth goes dry immediately.

"But I'd love to go first."

I can't look away. It's so ... beautiful. Thick and getting thicker every second. Long ... He's a shower *and* a grower. Two curved barbells —a double dydoe— adorn the crown of his cock.

"Sweets." His chest rumbles as he strokes down his cock then tugs on the silver balls on one side of his piercings.

I feel my knees wobble as I bend down, still eyeing his alluring manhood while pushing down my underwear.

"Damn," he hisses as he looks me over while sheathing himself.

"Damn," I mimic as I look him over too.

One step, his cock nudges my belly as he wraps his hand around the back of my neck. Our bodies fuse together as he crushes his lips against mine. Then he moves his hand to the base of my head as he licks his hot, wet tongue inside my mouth.

He tastes of mint and a hint of cigarette smoke. Never having kissed a smoker, it shocks me that I enjoy kissing... or, should I say, being kissed by one. I feel like I'm barely a part of this, like I'm there for his use in a way that's ... so damn amazing.

With his free hand, he takes mine from his hard chest and wraps it around his cock. I stroke him, and he groans into my mouth.

He slides his fingers down my belly and takes no time in pushing one inside of me as he growls against my lips. Then he moves his finger in and out of me slowly, and my head falls back with each tap to that spot no other man has found, even when given instruction.

He removes his hand from the back of my head as he slides his lips down my neck. Adding another finger, his mouth on my breast, my nails in his shoulders, my hips rotating, thrusting ...

"Oh my God."

"Don't you dare," he tugs on my nipple then sucks harshly. Releasing it with a *pop*, he looks up at me. "You lean back, you'll fuck up the art." Standing to his full height, he pulls his fingers out of me then turns me so my back is to him.

With his hand between my shoulder blades, I look back at him.

His demanding eyes penetrate me as he searches mine. "Gonna do you doggy, so your wrapping stays put."

Gonna do you doggy? A part of me feels like I should take a little offense to this. Oddly, no part of me actually does.

His eyes are now gone from mine as he looks over my naked body bent over the table. When they land on the art, as he calls it, his eyes flare then narrow, his jaw tightens and twitches as he curses, "Fuck."

"Fucking is when your dick is inside of me, and there's nothing between—"

My breath leaves my body as he slams into me.

He stills and hisses between clenched teeth, "I know what fucking is. Your pussy's so tight I'm thinking you're about to find out the true definition for the first time."

His magic fingers did nothing to prepare me. I'm painfully stretched but uncaring.

I narrow my eyes and attempt to keep my voice as even as I can when I challenge, "Why don't you get to it then?"

His smirk disappears. His eyes flash from mischief to lust, hazel to black. With his large inked hands, he grips my hips as I grip the edge of the table, preparing myself.

He pulls out slightly and slowly. Then, so, so slowly, he pushes in, and I swear his dick nudges my esophagus. His jaw tightens along with my insides as his eyes penetrate me as deeply as his cock.

"You gonna move, or should I take over?"

"You're gonna regret that question."

"You afraid you're going to bust a nut—"

He moves one hand from my hip and snakes it around my hair. He pulls me back and kisses me harshly, deeply. As I attempt to take over, he pulls away, his eyes menacing as he releases my hair. Then he swiftly moves his hand to my tit, squeezes it, and pinches my nipple.

It hurts, but fuck if it doesn't feel good, too.

"I have places to go, so you better ..." I stop when he removes his other hand from my hip and lifts my leg up, placing my knee on the table.

"You canceled your plans when you got naked with me."

I narrow my eyes, open my mouth, and then ... then he fucks me.

"Fuck!" I cry out.

Through his clenched teeth, he hisses, "That's right, sweets; this is fucking."

He fucks me hard, deep...*so good*. He plays with my tits and occasionally kisses me so hard I don't realize he's no longer kissing me when he does stop.

I cry out pleasures I've never cried before as he continues fucking me through one orgasm and into the next while I hang on to the table for dear life.

My body is no longer mine. It's completely and totally controlled by him as I reach places never reached before.

"Knees, sweets," he demands as he turns me around, fingers finding me again, not one, not two, but three as he kisses me unforgivingly again before pulling away and dragging his fingers from deep inside me to push down on my shoulder.

I sink willingly. If not, my legs would have given out at any moment without his controlling —puppeteering— fingers holding me up.

He pulls off the condom while hooking two fingers in my already gaping mouth and pulling me forward. "Put those lips I bruised around my cock, sweets."

I open wide, so fucking wide, and then he removes his fingers from my mouth to cup the back of my head as he fucks my face.

He steps back, forcing me to follow him as he turns our

bodies so he can sit on the table. I grip the base of him as he leans back, watching me now as I suck the saliva off his cock. His chest heaves, and his lips part slightly, his teeth still together.

"You better stop."

Feeling some sense of control now, I suck harder and pump faster as I watch him begin to lose it.

I give him a slow wink, and his brow rises.

Reaching down, he lifts me up as I bite down on him.

A deep rumble leaves his chest. "Good way to chip a tooth." He pulls me up as he leans back. "On my fucking face, sweet treat."

He doesn't wait for me to finish him off. He grips my hips and pulls me up.

I turn my body so that I can taste his soft, steel-like skin in my mouth as he pulls my soaked center onto his face and licks me savagely.

Against me, he groans, "Last warning."

I don't stop until I'm sure his face is covered with my juices, and my mouth is full of his cum.

Still swallowing ... trying to catch my breath and slow my heartbeat, I swing my leg over and dismount the face of a ... fucking man ... and try my best to stop my legs from shaking while I stand on the floor.

Awkward is never a feeling I've had after sex, but then again, I've never actually had sex with a person that I met just four hours ago.

Unsatisfied and questioning why I bothered getting naked for maybe ten minutes, if I was lucky, to race to the finish, a race I always lost. That was sex ... until twenty minutes ago.

As I begin to squat down to grab my haphazardly discarded clothing, a hand on my hip stops me. I begin to look back when I feel a warm cloth between my legs. I didn't even hear the water run.

"I'd offer you a shower, but ..." He leaves it hanging as he wipes up one thigh then the next before beginning to wipe my center.

"I can manage." I reach down and attempt to take the cloth, but he doesn't let go. I look back to see his eyes are softer now.

"Take your time."

"Take my time?" I ask.

"Getting your shit straight." He holds back a smirk.

"I assure you, my shit's straight." *My shit is* so *not straight.*

"If we had more time, I would have fucked that up, too." He steps back and looks me over.

The source of raw emptiness pulses again.

He makes no attempt to put clothes on; he simply watches me with irritating amusement.

"You do know I just fucked your face, so ..." I give him a smug look and shrug.

When he laughs, I arch a brow while pulling my underpants up.

He holds his hands up as if to mockingly concede, I turn my back to him as I put on my bra, trying to hide my own smile.

I just fucked your face? Really? I scold myself.

When I feel my tank top being placed over my head, I softly thank him and push my arms through the holes.

"How much do I owe you?"

"For fucking my face? That was my pleasure. No charge."

My elbow jerks back and hits the wall of muscles behind me lightly. He chuckles.

"The art."

"How about, when you come back in, we'll discuss it?"

I turn around and look up at him, careful to avert my eyes from the body of a god who is holding my skirt. "This was a hookup." I roll my eyes, trying to play it off that the thought of seeing him naked doesn't entice the swarm of butterflies in my belly that have begun to dance again, and grab my skirt hanging off fingers that were inside me minutes ago.

He quirks an eyebrow. "Six to nine months later doesn't exactly constitute a serious relationship."

"If I can squeeze you into the rotation, I'll let you know."

He bends down and grabs my sweater before I have a chance and holds it up. "Must be a small rotation, since I barely squeezed into you, sweets."

I push my arms into the sweater. "I've had"—I pause as he turns me around and steps back, pointing down with a very self-assured look on his face—"bigger."

"Hard or soft plastic?" he asks.

Both of us try not to laugh but fail.

I turn my back to him then grab my purse from the chair. "I'm paying for the service, not the fuck. How much?"

"I'm not taking your money." He turns his back to grab his clothes.

"I—"

"Sixty-nine dollars." He pulls his jeans up. He's smirking when he turns and looks at me as he pulls his shirt over his head.

I walk out of the room, shaking my head and biting back a laugh, but I unleash a grin. I reach into my purse and grab the envelope out of it from the money I pulled from the bank so Dad wouldn't see my purchase. Then I drop it onto the counter and walk to the door, where I unlock it, open it and leave.

OH MY FREAKING GOD! I silently scream as I hurry up the sidewalk, hoping to find a cab to take me back to The Empire so I can spill all the tea to my girls.

SIX
ARTISTIC EXPRESSIONS
TAGS

What the fuck am I doing? I ask myself as I run barefoot down the street after the sweet treat whose ass and sass I will not soon forget, holding the envelope she tossed on the counter.

She turns the corner, and I start to slow, knowing I've probably lost her, but then I decide, *fuck that.*

When I turn the corner, I spot her and try my best to slow down. She's got her nose in her phone and doesn't see me as I attempt to stop myself from running her over. Unable to stop completely, I grab her to make sure she doesn't fall.

She gasps and looks up at me. "Are you freaking insane?"

My back hits the trash can and stops my fall. "Undecided on a few occasions."

"What the hell are you doing?" She tries not to laugh then decides against holding it back.

She's so fucking beautiful that I decide not to hold back either, and I kiss her.

"Oh my freaking God," she mumbles against my lips.

I pull back, taking her bottom lip with me. When I release it, she shakes her head.

"You're insane."

"I told you not to pay until—"

She gasps and begins looking around. "My purse, my phone."

I hurry over to her purse and see a cab pulling over. With my back still to her, I shove the envelope inside then hurry back to her.

"I have friends waiting for me," she says, looking at me like she's confused. It's cute as fuck.

"I do, too," I say, opening the cab door for her. "Catch up in six to nine."

She laughs like I'm joking. I'm not.

"What's your name, sweets?"

She giggles. "Why?"

"Because I want to know the name of the girl I'll be beating off to until we meet again."

"Bella," she answers as she laughs at me.

I feel like I just got a knee to the gut. The breathlessness, not the pain. Same way I felt when she turned toward me the first time.

"Yours?"

"Miss, do you still need a ride?" the cab driver asks.

"Go. I'll see you around."

She slides in and looks out at me.

Fuck.

I shake my head.

She looks disappointed but shrugs then gives me a peace sign before grabbing the door and shutting it.

Fuck.

I take a step back as I watch the cab begin to pull away.

She turns and looks out the back window. I shoot her a

peace sign, and she smirks. Then I realize I didn't lock the shop, so I sprint back to make sure I do.

Bell, peace, freedom ... Bella. Paula is going to have a field day with this.

Which is why I will never fucking tell her.

* * *

WHEN I WALK into the twenty-four-hour fitness center, Sisco is at the counter, chatting it up with one of the girls.

"You're late as hell, man. I've already had a drink, eaten, and worked out." He laughs, giving me a bro hug. Stepping back, he then looks me up and down. "You dirty dog."

"I'm just gonna shower off before I go home so the old lady doesn't flip the fuck out on me."

"You got a ride?"

"Taking the Nike express home." I wink.

"You sure, man? I can wait."

"No. Great last day of freedom ended with one hell of a piece of *art*."

"I don't like that look, Tags."

"It's all good."

SEVEN
ASSHOLE(S)
BELLA

Of course, the greatest sexual experience of my life, with a man—well, I thought he was a man—who warmed me up and made me pop quicker than microwave popcorn, turned out to be a grade-A asshole.

When I found the money in my purse, I got all sorts of stupid.

I don't do stupid.

I also don't chase boys; I make them chase me. If they tire at all, take so much as a water break, they're out.

But this envelope, the one I am carrying, the one he gave me back on the sly, further heating my already hot and bothered self, is now going to be spent on drinks with my girls.

Why? Because I followed him from the shop to a twenty-four-hour fitness center, looking for the perfect time to slip the envelope in his bag, when I heard him tell his buddy, "I'm just gonna shower off before I go home so the old lady doesn't flip the fuck out on me."

I, Isabella Steel, not only fucked a hot tattoo artist, which was never on my list of things to do during college, and it literally makes me feel like I may throw up now, but I fucked a married one.

Walking from the bar out to the rooftop, I spot Victoria sucking face with Brian, her douchebag ex's roommate. Alice sitting on one of the many couches, and Lily is passed out with her head on Alice's lap.

Alice looks up and waves to me as I walk over.

"Let me see." She smiles broadly.

I pull my phone from my bag. "Take a picture for me?"

"Of course."

When I turn around and lift my shirt, she breathes in an exaggerated breath. "Beautiful."

I look over my shoulder. "Can you see it through the wrap?"

"Yes, it's so much bigger than I expected. And the flowers ... wow."

"Pic?" I remind her.

"Of course."

When she hands me back the phone, I walk over and sit on the couch beside Lily's ass.

"So, did it hurt?" she asks as I look at the picture and zoom in as far as I can.

I nod. "Yeah, it sure did."

I know beautiful body art, and even though its dark I can tell this is beautiful work.

"What was the artist like?" she asks.

Shaking my head, I flop back against the cushion. "Hot as hell. Hung, too."

"You ... you ..." She pauses then realization hits. "You ..."

I stop her from continuing. "I had a one-night stand."

"You mean"—she pauses and looks at her own phone —"five-hour stand."

I cringe at the thought. Then I cringe again at the thought that I was with a married man. My night was double cringeworthy.

"Which is much more daring than a full night." She is so sweet.

"Yeah." I smile and nod. "Well, I did it. I destroyed Dad's list of don'ts."

She waves over a waitress. "We need two glasses of your best champagne."

The waitress nods.

I pull out the envelope and hand it to her. "We'll take a whole bottle. Keep the change."

When the waitress leaves, Alice whispers, "You know I can't drink more than a glass or I get kind of crazy." Her bright blue eyes are sparkling under the red neon sign.

Alice's version of crazy is falling asleep.

I smile. "Then let's make our last night together really crazy."

Really crazy ends up with Alice drinking two glasses of wine and me polishing off the rest of the bottle.

Graduation day, we woke to my entire family—all of them—coming to our apartment, and all of us, except Alice, dragging ass while getting ready.

Dad was not impressed, but Carly kept him in check and he eventually chilled out.

We had dinner with Alice, Victoria, and Lily's families immediately after the ceremony and then, in true Steel family style, we were on a plane within an hour, heading to Savannah, Georgia to attend a wedding.

Never a dull moment.

* * *

STANDING ON MY SECOND COUSIN, Dominic's yacht, I have admittedly drank too much champagne … again. But it helps as I try not to think about … *What's his name?*

No, really, what is his name? I don't even remember.

I look at my phone and the picture of my tattoo, the one Alice took. Hell, I haven't even had enough private time in the bathroom by myself to get a good look at it.

My siblings, Kiki and Max, have been square up my ass. My roommates weren't ones to give much privacy, but they gave a hell of a lot more than my siblings and my cousins do. Besides, I wouldn't have to hide it from them.

I'm a freaking adult, dammit, and stuck in the middle of actually being treated like one and a child.

The kids, they missed me. I get it. I missed them, too. But Kiki is even in the bathroom when I shower. It's a freaking miracle she hasn't seen my art. My art that … a married freaking man put on my skin then fucked me so hard I'm still feeling it.

A married man.

I guess it's good that I'm stuck floating on the Atlantic Ocean or I may want to go find that big ~~beautiful~~ bastard and de-nut him with my freshly manicured claws. But, as Carly told me in middle school, after the biggest emotional pain I ever experienced as a teen, "We have two days to grieve, then we celebrate the lesson we learned from that person."

The biggest emotional pain was a breakup with my best friend. Yes, it was a breakup, worse than any breakup I've ever had. I found out she was talking behind my back and sharing pictures that she had no right even taking while at my house when she slept over.

The picture was of Dad cooking pancakes in his pajama

bottoms. It circulated all over my Catholic school. My real best friend, Laura, is the one who showed me. Then she showed me Danielle's finsta—fake Instagram account—called Hot Daddies. It was a year's worth of pictures that she had sneakily taken of my father and uncles while she was allowed to be part of my family.

It hurt. It hurt bad. The lesson I learned was something insurmountable: Loyalty isn't a given. Very few actually give it, and even fewer deserve it. She wasn't one of those people.

The bigger lesson? There aren't many who know what loyalty truly means. It's another way in which my family is so different. But this difference isn't one that annoys me. It's one I will always treasure.

It's been two days, and I am done slut-shaming myself. He's the married one, not me.

Now, I celebrate the lesson I learned: Look for a ring, ask if they're married, and don't just assume.

I shake two imaginary middle fingers and scream in my head, *Fuck you ... what's-your-name.*

The best way to get over him is to get under someone else, says my mix of badass and booze.

Luckily for me, I'm aboard the SS Hotness. Seriously, though, the waitstaff is pretty much a buffet of non-family members who look like they'd be a great place to start. Maybe not mount one, but a heavy make-out session would do the body good.

Turning away from the waiters and back to those still on the party deck, I realize this isn't going to be an easy task. I'm surrounded by my family, who I love, but already crave a moment away from, from time to time. Times like now, when the newlyweds, close family friends, Paige and Vincent, are on their own yacht far enough away from the one the rest of us are on, yet close enough to be a reminder of what is going on—consummation of vows—to remind one's drunken self that she has needs, too. Needs met two days ago ... that *need* to be washed away with the tide.

My two days grieving period will be over, and I will have already chalked it up to ... one hell of a night that I hope to soon forget.

God, that sounds so weak, and I'm not weak. But really? Why does the only man who ever got me have to be a married one? And why does semi-sober me ignore six to nine months? Really? He *is* probably going to freaking jail!

No matter. It's over and I have needs. Needs that I must ignore because of the fact that I'm stuck in Steel purgatory, somewhere between the adults and Steel generation next.

With my younger siblings and cousins fast asleep in the dining hall, cleared out for our "family sleepover" on the yacht, the same damn room they expect me, an independent, young college graduate to sleep in, I should feel free to act my age. Times like now when my dad, Momma Carly, all my aunts, uncles, and family friends—all couples—are out of their wedding attire and in casual clothes or swimwear, dancing, drinking, and you know damn well they will all be fucking soon. Hell, even Momma Joe and Thomas aren't making room for Jesus as they grind against each other to the beat of the music.

Times like now, when across the deck, leaning against the railings, stands a man who is sexy as hell and, most importantly, unrelated. He's got to be one of the waitstaff, and he's probably thinking I'm some spoiled, rich brat who would never give him the time of day.

He's wrong.

I would not only give him the time of day; I'd let him have some of my night.

Now, to figure out how to avoid Dad. Clearly, I'm no virgin, but he has it in his head that I am. He doesn't have any clue that I had a boyfriend in college, who I hid from my family for obvious reasons. He'd be dead, and they'd be in jail. And by *they*, I mean Dad.

I've had my rebound fuck ... and he's not allowed in my head anymore. But I can't make it stop. There is no way he could have been that good. I'm sure it was the fact that I'd had Danny for so long that taking in some *strange*, and the way in which it all went down, was what really got me off.

No matter. He doesn't deserve me, and now I'm going to find something to take the taste of him ... out of my mouth.

I drink the rest of the champagne in my glass, watching the man watching me. Then I reach behind me and pat the itch on my back caused by the tattoo I'm hiding.

She is beauty ... She is wisdom ... She is strength ... She is love ... She is me.

My idea. *Mine*, not his.

Beauty represents my mother, who died while giving birth to me. In the pictures, she is younger than I am now, and she is stunning. Everyone tells me I look just like her, except for the fact that I have my father's coloring, and she was ... is blonde.

Wisdom is my maternal grandmother, who raised me from the day I was born until she died when I was eight. Everything she taught me is still remembered, and as I get older, I realize that each "lesson" was something that was relevant then and has continued to be.

Strength represents Momma Joe, who doesn't let anything hold her back or hold her down. She pushes forward no matter what this harsh, cruel world has done to hold her. She pushes forward, and not just for her but for all of us.

Love, love is Momma Carly. From everything I have seen or heard, or been a part of, she is the epitome of love.

I can't wait until things aren't crazy, meaning I can't wait to move into my own place so I can be alone in the bathroom, or my own room, for that matter, without Kiki or Max busting in.

"Soon," I say on a sigh. "Very soon."

I watch as they all start disappearing by twos until only Dad and Carly are still dancing.

I love the way they look at each other. I laugh while thinking about how he can be so angry at her one minute for doing something to make him that way. It's always something non-life-threatening, but by his reaction, you'd think otherwise. Yet, he never stops looking at her the way he is now. Someday, I hope I can have that.

Love.

Until then, something that feels kind of like love will work.

When Dad and Carly are gone, I make my way to the bar, which happens to be exactly halfway between me and the hot man ... Or, at least I hope he's as hot as I think; it *is* dark.

I place my empty glass on the bar, laughing to myself again while thinking, *If he's not really that hot, the champagne will make him appear that way.*

Holding up two fingers, I tell the bartender, "Two please."

I drink the first one down just in case he's not that good-looking then set down the flute and grab the other. I'm starting to turn around when I look up and see the man I've been ogling for the past hour standing right next to me.

"I thought maybe that one was for me." The side of his mouth turns upward slightly in a smile. I swear his teeth sparkle as he looks away and nods to the bartender, holding up two fingers.

I swipe my tongue over my teeth, hoping they'll sparkle like his do. "I would have, but I wasn't sure if you were part of the cast or crew."

He turns and leans against the bar, taking a drink before asking, "Which are you?"

"Crew, of course. Just like you." I raise my glass and wink.

Now, it's really not a lie. This is indeed quite a crew.

I drink slower now, not wanting to be totally inebriated, because this man is hot, like seriously hot, and also the polar opposite of ... what's-his-name. I want to remember this one.

He has a full head of dark blond hair, blue eyes, a day or two worth of stubble covering his jaw, and a body that is definitely rocking the black V-neck, khaki cargo shorts, and flip flops.

I see him eyeing me the same as I am him, taking me all in.

I am in a Dad-approved swimsuit, even though I can't go swimming for a while. The top isn't all that revealing, which of course makes Dad happy, and the bottoms ... well, I'm wearing a wrap for a reason.

When his eyes finally make their way up to mine, he asks, "You thinking about going for a swim?"

I set my glass down and smile. "I've been thinking about a lot of things."

His smile grows. "Is that so?"

I shrug. "Weren't we both?"

He looks me over again, slower this time, his eyes darkening, yet he says nothing.

No matter. It is what it is ... God, I hope it is.

My mouth is suddenly dry, so I drink down the rest of the champagne, for courage this time, and then set the empty on the bar. "I'm going to take a walk toward the back of the boat." I place my hand against his waist, and I smile inwardly when I feel how hard his abs are. Abs, I love abs. "I might get thirsty."

He licks his lips, eyes cast downward, looking at my chest.

I step back and turn around, allowing him to take in more of my *ass*ets. I look over my shoulder and give him the sultriest look I can pull off then slowly walk away.

I hear him behind me ... and so do my nipples.

He's hot. *So* hot. Definitely hotter than Danny and maybe even hotter than ... *what's his name?*

I slow down, allowing him to catch up. He swings his arm around me from behind, a glass of champagne in his hand.

I stop and look behind me. He's looking down at me with beautiful eyes.

I tip my head back and close my eyes as his lips come closer to mine ...

"What the fuck do you think you're doing young—"

I turn my head quickly and groan, "Daddy, go away!"

The arm in front of me quickly disappears as Dad stomps toward me. I look past him, knowing Carly will make him ... behave, but she's not there.

Dammit!

"—really fucking young, lady."

Buzzed and pissed, I decide to take care of the situation the way I was taught to handle my *shit* ... by him!

Rule number one: Make sure you're right before you start some shit.

I know I'm right. I'm of legal age!

Rule number two: Be confident enough to handle your shit.

So, I go with that.

I hit him with rule number one, holding up my hand and telling him, "Dad, I'm of legal age to drink."

"Dad?" I hear tall, blond, and gorgeous snarl from behind me.

Dad's about to say something, so I hit him with rule number two.

"To be clear, I'm an adult, so this"—I motion between me and ... aw hell, I don't know his name either—"is none of your business."

"You will always be my fucking business, *Little* Bell." He points at me then at the hottie. "And what the fuck are you thinking, Arnesen?"

Arnesen? Oh damn, he's Paige's, the bride's, brother.

"I was thinking she was thirsty," he snaps back at Dad.

I cringe. *Oh, here we freaking go.*

"I was also *not* thinking she was one of you." If he had said that with less attitude, it would have defused the situation, but he clearly isn't intimidated by my father.

Stow it before I blow it, is not only Dad's warning, but his exact words whenever I pop off at the mouth at him. I never pushed hard enough to see what him *blowing it* actually meant.

Time to diffuse the ticking time bomb that is Jase Steel.

"It was an honest mistake," I say, hoping to catch his attention because Dad is turning red — I can even tell in the dim lighting— and his fists are actually balled-up at his sides. If I think about it, he truly resembles a cartoon character who is actually ready to explode into a million confetti-colored pieces.

He doesn't look at me, but *Arnesen* gives me a sideways scowl, and yes, I know I shouldn't have lied.

I attempt to step between them when Dad grabs my arms, moves me aside, and then demands, "Get your ass to bed."

He isn't stepping away, and Arnesen isn't either.

Time to do the right thing or, in this case, the wrong thing to ensure there is no fight and that my overbearing father doesn't do something because his grown-ASS, adult daughter is going to act her age.

Ass. Huh, that'll surely work.

"I'm going for a swim first."

I'm definitely not going for a swim.

I untie my wrap and let it drop to the ground before quickly starting to walk away.

"You aren't going ... What in the fuck did you do!"

"Jase!" I hear Carly yell, and then I see her running down the deck.

"What? This?" I ask as I reach behind me and point to my ink.

"Which one of those motherfuckers did that without asking permission!"

"Jase." Carly stands between us, panting as she tries to catch her breath.

"No, nope, no way, baby. This is some bullshit." Dad moves her to the side and starts coming toward me. "Who fucking did that to you?"

I don't think I've ever seen him so angry. It's scary ... really scary.

"I had it done when I was in New York."

"You go to some fucking shop in New York and let someone ink you? A tramp stamp, Isabella?"

When he grabs my arm, I see Paige's brother step toward us. Carly does, too.

She grabs his arm, stopping him. "Pace, she's fine."

Pace. His name is Pace.

Again, in true cartoon fashion, Dad's eyes bug out of his head as he whips around to look at ... *Pace*. "And what the fuck do you think you're gonna do, asshole?"

"Jase, that's enough," Carly says as Pace glares at my dad.

I pull my arm away from my father while he's side-tracked, and he snaps his head back toward me.

I hold up my hand, stopping him from saying a thing while I begin to speak. "I asked you, and you told me no several times. It means a lot to me; just like yours do. And Dad, it's pretty fu—"—I stop when his eyebrows nearly jump up and off his face then groan as his constant and obvious hypocrisy shines through ... again—"messed up that you are covered in them yet tell me I can't. That you can curse yet freak when I do. I'm a grown-ass woman, Dad."

"You fucking think so?" he snaps.

"No, Dad, I know so! And I know damn well Momma Joe never gave you half the crap you give me. She let you make your own choices; learn as you grew and matured. So give me the same courtesy, would you?"

He throws his hands in the air. "You got a fucking tramp stamp!"

I refuse to tell him that ... what's-his-name talked me into the placement. And I refuse to point out the obvious—it's not a tramp stamp.

"'*She is beauty ... She is wisdom ... She is strength ... She is love ... She is me*'. That's what it says, Dad. It represents all the women in my life who have influenced me. It means so much to me. My mom, Grandma Charlotte, Momma Joe, and Carly. It represents them being a part of me."

For a moment, I can see how it affects him, but then he's back to pissed.

"The women?" he huffs.

"I could always get an arrow pointing to the crack of my ass with the words *'He Is An'* above it, Dad."

When Carly snorts, Dad looks back and snarls at her.

"I'm sorry, Jase, but that was hilarious."

He rolls his eyes, throws his hands in the air, and then looks back at me. "Get your ass to bed."

With my buzz wearing off and knowing my father isn't going to leave this alone, I sigh as I bend over to pick up my wrap. Then I walk past him and stop in front of Pace. "I'm sorry I wasn't honest about being part of the cast and not the crew, but as you can see"—I throw my thumb back toward my dad—"it's sometimes a necessary evil."

Pace nods. "If you were my daughter, I can't say I'd be any different."

"And she could be," Dad sputters.

I roll my eyes and begin to walk away. "Night."

Carly rushes up and stops me by taking my hand. "I think the thought behind your tattoo is beautiful."

I can't help hugging her any more than I can help feeling emotions building up behind my eyes as I whisper, "You're love."

"Oh Bell, so are you." She hugs me tightly then steps back and smiles. "Can I see?"

A smile bursts out of me as I hand her my phone, excited that I no longer have to hide it and can finally show someone. "Can you take a picture for me so I can get a better look?"

"Of course."

When Carly walks behind me, she clears her throat.

"Um, what did you say it says?"

" '*She is beauty ... She is wisdom ... She is strength ... She is love ... She is me*'."

"Oh dear," she whispers.

Hearing the concern in her voice, I look back at her. She's looking at my tattoo, cringing ever so slightly.

EIGHT
THUGS
BELLA

Lying in the dining hall on an air mattress, amongst my siblings and cousins, I feel sick. And not because the water is rocking the yacht, because that is actually the only thing comforting to me right now. But because I have a tattoo on my lower back that I have pondered for years, and it's now tainted by the artist who I have vowed to myself that I would find and castrate as soon as I get off this boat.

I hold up my phone one last time and look at the picture of what he did to me. The art is beautiful. Dare I say more detailed than I think I've ever seen?

Let's be honest; I don't dare. That's why I'm thinking it ... in my head.

But he tainted it.

She is beauty ... She is wisdom ... She is strength ... She is love ... She is mine.

"No, motherfucker, I am mine!" I hiss at the picture.

"Huh?"

I look up and get blinded by a flashlight in my face.

"Kiki, you're blinding me."

She turns it off. "Sorry." Then she crawls over to me and sits on my air mattress. "Did you just say motherfucker?"

"Language," I scold, sounding just like Dad.

"Look around, Bell; you're no more an adult than we are. So, if I wanna say motherfucker, I will say motherfucker."

I'm completely shocked. "Oh my God, Kiki. Really?"

In the dark, from a distance, I hear a whispered *motherfucker* against stifled giggles. Then another whispered *motherfucker*, followed by more giggles and many ... many more *motherfuckers*. I feel like I'm camping in the middle of a field, but instead of being surrounded by crickets, I'm surrounded by all the little Steels chirping *motherfucker* and giggling.

"Enough!" I whisper-hiss at them as I turn on my phone light and flash it around the room, seeing all their faces grinning. "That's enough."

Then, like little cockroaches, they begin to crawl toward me. When I'm completely circled by Max, Truth, Justice, Patrick, Tris, Amias, and Brisa, I look at Kiki and arch my brow. "See what you've done?"

Oh my God, I am now acting their age.

She says nothing. It's fucking creepy.

When Justice turns on his phone light so it points up at his face, it's even creepier. When they all follow suit, I pull my sleeping bag up to my chin.

Justice narrows his eyes. "We made a decision."

"Is that so?"

"Yeah." Max scowls. "You need to Steel up."

"Steel up?" I ask, trying to hide my amusement.

"They kept saying man up, and we decided it was sexist," Truth explains.

"Meaning, you need to grow a set," Kiki clarifies, as if I need her to.

"The way we see it, we've let you lead the way long enough, Bell. No disrespect, but you keep it up, I'll be yanking my chain well into my twenties, and I am *so* sick of you yanking my chain," Patrick huffs.

They all look from him to me.

"You got a tattoo, and you come running in here like you're still in middle school," Amias states matter-of-factly. "You're a woman. A beautiful woman who needs to own her womanhood."

Oh my God, he sounds just like Uncle Zandor.

His sister Tris pipes in with, "I don't plan to be a virgin throughout high school."

"She's not sad because she's a virgin, Tris; she's sad because someone gave her a tattoo and botched it up," Brisa tells her sister, and then they all look at me.

"Is it bad?" Justice asks.

"It's fine," I lie, trying to stop the madness and questions. "Nothing any of you—"

" '*She is mine.*' Someone tagged her ass," Patrick snaps, "without consent."

"How the hell do you know that?"

"I was tailing Aunt Carly, hiding behind the post."

What the fuck?

"This is none of your business," I scold him.

"Two things," Justice begins. "One, you're wrong. What you do affects us. Two, I want his name and address, because that's fucked up, Bell, and he needs to learn a lesson."

I laugh. "And what are you going to do about it?"

"We," Kiki pipes in. "What are *we* gonna do about it."

Oh, my good Lord, if Dad thinks I'm hard to handle, he's in for a rude awakening.

Max grins. "We're gonna teach him a big-ass lesson."

I can't help laughing at that. "Oh yeah? And what are you gonna do? You can't even drive."

They all look at Patrick, who gives them all a death glare.

"Please tell me you, at fifteen, haven't driven. That's illegal and unsafe, Patrick."

"That's neither here nor there," Kiki draws the attention away from a completely horrifying realization.

"We'll just rough him up," Amias states.

"Tag him," Tris adds.

"It'll be done quietly, and no one will—"

"Hell no." Not gonna lie, I'm a little more than concerned now. I don't know if they're letting their imaginations fly or if they really would try to do something like this. "You'll be kids. Nice kids. Nice Catholic school kids who—"

"Can you imagine how terrified the asshole is going to be when we all come for him?" Patrick laughs.

"In Catholic school uniforms?" I scold him. "He's a man, not a kid. And—"

"You ever see *Children of the Corn*, Bell?" Max asks. "Kids can be fucking terrifying."

I have to do something, because they look serious as shit.

"He's my boyfriend."

They all gasp.

Shit, shit, shit.

"He was, and then we broke up."

I am going to Hell, but as I look around, I realize the chances are slim that I won't be alone for long.

Kiki grins. "Does Dad know?"

I shake my head.

She flashes her phone around to each of their faces. "We keep this between us."

They all grumble.

She narrows her eyes. "We use it when we need it, but she's one of us." Then she looks back at me. "You really need to stop being such a pussy."

"Doesn't mean we don't love you, but really? You just got your Masters." Max looks at me like I'm the child and he's not before he walks back to his mattress.

Tris smiles. "What was sex like?"

"You're like ten," I scold her.

"I'm like twelve." She rolls her eyes and stands up then looks down at me. "And I've already been felt up."

I lose my shit.

"All you motherfuckers back here right fucking now!"

They jump, and I get a slight bit of satisfaction from it. Then they all come back.

"Sit." I point down and, oddly, they do. "Rules were made for other reasons than breaking. You break them for fun, then you're a bunch of little thugs. You break them because they're ridiculous, that's another thing."

"Well, Dad's rules are ridiculous," Kiki interrupts.

I point at her. "You be quiet and listen. No dating, no drinking, no drugs, and no decorating. Dad may be over the top, but he made them for a reason."

"Mainly because he broke every fucking one of them," Kiki quips.

"I'm adding one. No being dumb. You sound dumb when you say fuck every other word, not adult."

"It's a great word," Max, my thirteen-year-old brother, defends her. "Very versatile."

"Okay, Max, go ahead and play the dumb card even

harder. But it's true. Spend a little less time trying to be a thug and a little more time broadening your vocabulary."

I look at Tris. "No boy deserves to touch your twelve-year-old boobs."

"It's not about the boy. My boobs deserve to be touched and admired," she replies flippantly.

"Dear God, they haven't even fully checked in yet! They're at an awkward stage. And," I huff, "*And,* you ever look at a penny from the 60s?"

She looks at me like I'm nuts.

"They've been handled enough that they lost their luster. You want your tits to look like a worn penny before they are even fully developed?"

She looks horrified, and I feel bad that I'm full of shit ... but only a little.

"You all think I'm being a pussy? Well, guess what. I'm not. I'm the OG of this little crew, and you need to remember and respect that position. No dating until you're at least sixteen. And even though some of you are close, hang tight. No drinking because it's illegal, not because it's your parents' rules. No drugs; same as drinking, and it's stupid to trust anyone who hands you a pill, powder, or something to smoke—you don't touch it. You don't know their intentions. And no decorating because you have no clue if what you put on your body is something you'll want forever."

I watch them all look at each other.

"What? What have you already done?"

Patrick, Kiki, Truth, and Justice hold up their middle fingers.

"Oh, real mature. And you—"

"Decorating," Max says. "When we're thirteen, we get inked."

"By who!" I gasp.

I catch their sideways glance at Justice, and then they all put their hands back down.

After several moments, Justice shines his light on the inside of his middle finger, and I see the words *Forever Steel*.

"You all have these?" I ask.

The four of them nod.

"And Justice did it?"

Only Justice nods.

"It's against their rules," I scold them.

They hold eye contact, none letting out the unspoken *tough shit* words fly around in their adolescent minds, but I see them.

I cave, "But not mine."

"You won't tell?" Kiki asks.

"Not if he does mine when we get back home."

They look relieved.

They aren't getting off that easily.

"If I had to live by them, so do you. At least until you're of age. And then, you talk to me, to each other, and if all else fails, you call in the big guns."

"Momma Joe," they all say together.

"And seriously, drugs are for thugs, and we're not thugs."

"We're Steel." Justice nods.

"We're Steel," I agree.

"If we agree to this," Kiki draws my attention back to her, "you gotta agree to live your life the way you want it and not how they expect."

"I have been, Kiki, and I've done it by respecting them enough to live by the core of their rules, their values. You do the same."

"But you're going to work with them, not do what you went to school for?" Max asks. "The TV thing?"

"I'm going to work for them until a better opportunity comes up," I whisper as I sit back down. "The job market is tough, and I'm grateful I have a job right out of college. I'm thankful I have my education paid for, which they did for me by working hard. And I'm thankful I have all of you. I'm not giving up on my dreams. I'm waiting for something spectacular."

"Well, promise us you'll look, because we all have dreams, you know," Kiki states. "And if you don't do that, the rest of us are going to have one fu ... heck of a time when we're up."

* * *

I'M STILL awake when they all finally pass out. It's a wonder the rest of the kids didn't wake up. I suspect they were pretending to be asleep. If they heard me, oh well; it's not like they didn't need to hear it, too.

I wait a few more moments then reach for my bag. I pull out my sweatshirt and a pair of leggings, throw them on, and then pull my swimsuit top off from under it and toss it aside. I then grab the small bag containing my toothbrush and toothpaste, facial toilettes, moisturizer, and the ointment and cleanser to take care of my tattoo.

When I walk out, I see them all sitting in lounge chairs on the deck outside the dining room. Dad, Cyrus, Zandor, Xavier, Abe, Dominic, Sabato, Franco, and Pace.

Shit.

I turn left and see Carly, Tara, Bekah, Taelyn, Nikki, Laney, Melyssa, and Momma Joe.

"Not quite a united front," I joke as I walk between

them, thinking about the movie The Green Mile and expecting them all to yell out, "*Dead Man Walking.*"

Dad stands. "Who's the thug who tagged you, Bella?"

I freeze, having no idea what to say. If I say I don't know, I look like the asshole that I am. If I answer honestly, Dad's going to jail.

"Me."

I look left as Momma Joe stands.

"With all due respect, Momma Joe, bullshit."

"With all due respect, it's my adult decision to make, just like hooking up with him would have been." I point a finger at Pace.

Pace runs a hand up and down his face.

"You don't hookup!" Dad snaps.

"I did six years of college, managed to make the Dean's list every semester, and graduated with honors. I'm sorry to disappoint you, Dad, I may have left home at eighteen with my V-card, but it got punched a few times. Now, it's late. I'm going to take care of my tattoo, and then I'm going back to the kiddie pool. And by the way, you need to sway your focus from me to them. I was a cake walk in comparison to what you all have going on in there." That said, I hurry to get away from them and find a bathroom.

Standing in front of the mirror, I wash my face and am not at all surprised when Dad walks in.

"You love him 'cause he's ink next to the women you love, a part of you forever now."

"It can be fixed if I don't."

He leans against the wall and looks at my reflection in the mirror as I apply moisturizer.

"When can I beat him?"

"Beat him?" I gasp.

"I mean meet. When can I meet the boy who marked the skin that was mine to protect?"

"How about half past *never*?"

I hear a giggle from outside.

Dad rolls his eyes. "Carly, get in here."

Thank God, I think to myself.

She walks in, and I see all the others standing behind her.

"Christ, really?" Dad snarls.

"The men are waiting for a name. The women want to hear about the man who Bella is dating." Carly smiles. "You may want to protect her body; we want to teach her how to deal with men like you."

"Men like us?" Dad and my uncles huff.

"Oh, most definitely," Tara pipes in. "We can't wait to meet him."

"They broke up," Bekah whispers.

"Yeah right." Carly laughs. "Been there, done that, and—"

"Baby, not now." Dad shakes his head.

"I think you should give her space. It's late," Momma Joe interjects.

"Yeah, Jase, it's late." Carly smiles a sloppy, I've-had-a-few-too-many-drinks kind of smile.

He looks at her then at me, and then his eyes dart back to her and widen.

I brush my teeth, and spit in the sink as I watch the way they look at each other, in the mirror. If it weren't my parents, it would be swoony.

I continue brushing.

"Go. You can grill me later for information you're not going to get."

Dad's eyes leave Carly and narrow at me. "I could pass

that around every fucking shop in New York and see whose book it's in. Easily find out who the asshole is."

Carly grabs his hand. "But you won't."

"And it's not in a book. It was done freehand, his design."

"No shit?" Xavier pushes into the tiny room. "Lemme see that."

"You kidding me, X?" Dad snaps.

"No, not at all." He laughs then looks at my reflection as I spit the rest of the paste out in the sink. "You mind?"

Sucking the water off my toothbrush, I lift the back of my shirt.

"Damn." Xavier nods then looks up. "Looks ..." He stops and laughs. "Free hand?"

I nod as I wipe my mouth.

Zandor leans in and laughs. "He may be better than—"

"Watch it, asshole," Dad snaps.

Zandor laughs. "Check the ego. I was talking about Cyrus."

Well, his son sure caught the bug, I think.

"You ever miss it?" Tara asks Cyrus, I'm assuming.

"Every day," Cyrus states. Then he leans in the doorway and looks at my back. "You like this guy, Bella?"

For four hours, I liked him a lot.

"I did."

"And now you don't?" He asks confused.

I don't even know his name. I laugh at how pathetic that sounds even in my own head. But I'm playing a game, so I shrug as I start to wash the spot on my back where he now resides permanently.

"Easy, Bella." Dad sighs, taking the damp cloth from me and gently swiping over it.

Now I want to cry.

"You need to let this heal, then I'll fix it."

Silence hangs over us like a lead balloon.

I look in the mirror at everyone's shocked expressions.

"She is, dot, dot, dot—like the others—then *me*, not *mine*, that good?" His eyes meet mine as he reaches over and grabs the ointment, and I nod. "Gonna have to carry it for a few months, then I fix it."

A tear falls down my face as he turns me around.

"No decorating, Bella. That last D is the one that tends to leave the biggest mark."

You're not kidding, I think.

"I should have done it when you asked. I'll bear the burden, but you don't do that shit again."

"You're not the easiest person to talk to."

"I get that." He hugs me. "This doesn't mean I'm not pissed, Little Bell."

And I get that, I think.

"I'm tired." I step back.

He looks me over and nods. "We can talk tomorrow."

"About what?" I shake my head.

"About the assholes I need to fuck up who touched you."

"Dad, really? I thought—"

"I'm your father," he says sternly.

"And I'm *your* daughter," I retort just as sternly.

"And good luck to both of you." Momma Joe laughs from outside.

NINE
NEW POSITION
BELLA

The last day of our trip, I avoided everyone by faking sick. I wasn't physically, but emotionally, I was a ball of stress. The plane ride home, I did the same thing. Have been for a couple days. And now, as I lie in my bed, I feel even worse.

When someone knocks on the door then opens it, I roll to my side so that my back faces them.

"Hey, you." It's Carly. "Are you feeling any better?"

I sit up and turn toward her. "I'm fine."

She sits down and hands me a plate with a sandwich on it.

I take the plate. "Thanks, Momma Carly."

"You're upset and avoiding your father. You're not too young to hear this. He and I had a rough start. I feel your pain Bella. I'm hear if you need a nonjudgmental ear."

"I'm avoiding him because I really don't like disappointing him, but also because I want to karate kick him off that high horse of his."

"I un—"

"And I don't want to karate kick him because you two are going to have your hands full with Kiki and Max."

She sighs. "Oh, we already do."

"Like seriously—"

"We heard what you said to all of them. Not the whispered part, but the part where you yelled at them." She smirks. "God, I wish I knew the rest, but I understand there are things you just don't tell your parents and, contrary to what your father thinks, it's not some new age bullshit. It's part of growing up."

"I'm aware it's not new age bullshit, Carly."

I look at Dad as he walks in. He sits on the bed and reaches for the other half of my sandwich.

Carly bats his hand away. "You ate."

"Baby, I will paddle your ass if you do that shit again," he replies jokingly, leaning against the headboard, and then he looks at me. "I'm proud of you, Bella, but that ink pisses me off."

"Everything pisses you off," I say with my mouth full to drive the point home. He doesn't like us talking with our mouths full.

He clenches his jaw, ensuring he doesn't give me any more ammunition.

"I'm a grown woman."

"Still my little Bell. The same girl—"

"Please don't."

He huffs and runs his hand through his hair. "That's who you are to me and always will be."

"And you're always going to be my dad, but seriously, your job is done. You did good, if I dare say so myself."

He smirks, trying to hide it by running his hand over his face. Then he looks at me. "A father's job is never done. And some punk—"

"My choice," I half-lie.

We stare at one another.

"If I ever need you to kick an ass, I'll let you know."

"Dad!" Max yells. "Dad!"

I smile. "Max needs you."

"Max needs an ass kicking." He smirks.

"DAD!"

"Oh, for fuck's sake," he grumbles as he pushes himself off my bed, leans down, and kisses my forehead. "We'd planned two days at the beach, but you can't go in the water for two weeks. It's an open wound, Bella."

"We can still go to the beach; I just can't go in the water."

He nods once. "We can hit Wildwood instead. Ride some rides."

"I'm good with the beach."

"You sure?" Carly asks.

"Of course."

"Then Monday, it's Steel Inc. And for real this time, no internship."

I nod because that's a fight for another day.

* * *

LYING on my stomach under the cabana that Dad rented, my phone rings.

I lift it and look at the screen. I can't really see it because of the sun's glare, but I hit *accept* anyway.

"Hello?"

"Isabella Steel?"

"This is she."

"This is David Gorgon, executive producer of *50 Shades of Ink*."

I can't help chuckling at the name of the show and how everyone seems to feed off E.L. James's success from the

Fifty Shades of Grey trilogy. I hope she gets royalties from all of those who do.

He continues without pause, "You were on our list of candidates for production assistants, and because you didn't really look the part, we moved down the list."

Asshole, I think.

"We had a position become available today and would like to give you the opportunity."

Holding back my excitement I say as calmly as possible, "I appreciate it."

"You may not when you meet the assholes you'll be working with. It's not an easy job. It's badass men who don't play all that well with others, all pitted against each other, which makes for an occasional unhappy workplace."

"I know how to deal with badass tattoo types."

He laughs. "I'm not sure you know what you're agreeing to, sweetheart, but your references seem to think you're an ass-buster. If you're willing, get yourself to Miami; we need you here tonight, ready for tomorrow."

Sitting up, I can't contain the excitement. "Will you shoot me an email with the details?"

"Doing it ..." He pauses. "Done."

"Thank you so much, Mr. Gorgon."

He laughs. "I hope you're still thanking me when it's all over by the first of the year."

"I appreciate the opportunity."

"We appreciate the acceptance. We'll give you a couple of the easier cast members to produce."

"I'd prefer to go balls deep, sir."

He chuckles. "You really don't want that, Isabella."

Looking at my father and uncles playing full contact frisbee, I smile. "I think you'd be surprised at just how much I can deal with."

"You pull this off, and I can guarantee you'll have a job with us until you look in the mirror and think, *what the hell am I living like this for?*" He laughs.

I hear commotion in the background.

"For fuck's sake!" he snaps. "I have an issue to take care of. See you later, Isabella."

"See you later, Mr. Gorgon."

Hanging up, I jump up and scream, "Yes! Yes! Yes!"

The "crew" all come running with looks of concern in their eyes. Annoying but adorable.

I grab Kiki and hug her. "I got a job."

"You got a job." She looks skeptically hopeful.

"I got a job!" I shake her.

"You got a job?" Max beams.

I pull him into a hug. "I got a job!"

"You got a job?" It's Brand Falcon, friends of the family's teenage son.

I pull him in and hug him. "I got a job!"

"You hug me any closer, I'm gonna give you a new one."

I push him away.

"Sorry, Bella, but you're just so fucking hot."

The little shit, who is now taller than me, has crushed on me for as long as I can remember. He has even serenaded me at family/friend gatherings and told people he was going to marry me. I would be flattered, if not for the fact that he's seventeen and, due to the fame, his head has grown too big for his cowboy hat—he's since begun sporting a backward baseball cap.

As Truth hugs me and whispers, "You did it," I watch Kiki scowl at Brand then at me. As long as he's crushed on me, she's crushed on him.

Releasing Truth, I pull Kiki in. "You know I don't like

him. You should also know he doesn't deserve your energy." I step back and look at her. She smirks.

"Now that's a fantasy." Brand chuckles. "Two at once."

Out of nowhere, Max lunges at him, and they both fall to the ground. Brand is laughing as Max shakes him.

"You got a better chance at the reality of my dick being shoved in your ass than that, Falcon."

Brand attempts to hold back a laugh, but it's a failed attempt.

Max pulls back his arm, fist balled.

"Max, no!" I yell.

Justice grabs his elbow and jacks him back. "Let it be. And Max, don't threaten a dude with a dick in the ass."

I see Patrick walk by Brand and kick sand in his face.

"What the hell's going on?" Dad runs up, followed by Cyrus, Zandor, Xavier, Gage and Garrett Falcon.

"Bella got a job." Tris claps.

Smiling, I look up at Dad ... and he's not smiling.

* * *

BACK IN THE HOTEL ROOM, Dad reads over the email with the attached itinerary as I toss clothes in my suitcase.

"Salary sucks, Bella. I'll double it."

"I need more clothes," I say, trying to ignore him.

"Miami; Las Vegas; Richmond, Virginia?" He pauses then continues, "Flint, Michigan; Portland; Austin, Texas; San Francisco."

Kiki brings in an armload of clothes. "Take these."

I give her a one-armed hug. "Thanks, Kiki."

"How the fuck do you go from Honolulu, Hawaii to Kansas City, Missouri?"

"I'm guessing a plane, Dad," I say as I shove more clothes in my bag.

"Los Angeles, and then to Philly?"

"Oh my God, this is amazing!" Kiki laughs.

"Bella, you need to think about this."

"What's to think about?" I ask as I walk past him and into the suite's bathroom. "It's going to be hosted online in hopes of getting picked up by a network. Either way, Dad, it's experience, a step toward my dream."

"Which is?"

I speak out, "Producing and directing meaningful and thought-provoking TV. Art, Dad. It's art."

Momma Joe walks in. "Flight booked. We have two hours to get you to the airport."

"Two fucking hours?" Dad gasps.

I look at Kiki and whisper, "I know where you get it from."

"The bad attitude? My controlling nature?" She smirks.

I roll my eyes. "The need to use the F-bomb in every sentence."

"Reality TV, Bell? That's thought-provoking?"

"Sure is. Who would have thought people would sit on their asses and watch the Kardashians get richer and richer, all the while wanting to be them and never putting in the work?" Kiki laughs.

"Language, Kiki," Dad scolds her.

"And I see where you get it from, too," she states while putting my toiletries in my carry-on case.

"My good looks? My unwavering and fierce focus on goals?" I ask.

"No, your need to correct my language." She rolls her eyes.

I take the case and smile at her. "I love you. And seriously, Kiki, you're too pretty to talk like that."

Carly walks in with a bag. "Bought you some badass gear to blend in."

I hug her. "You're the best."

"It's going to take an hour and a half to get to the airport with good traffic; we need to go." She smiles sadly.

"Fuck." Dad sighs. "Nothing like ripping the Band-Aid off a still bleeding wound."

I walk out and smile. "I just have to say, I think I have more faith in your parenting than you do."

He raises his eyebrows.

"I think you did one hell of a job raising a daughter who busted her butt to get where she wants to be. I think you should celebrate the fact that your oldest child got a job that you know she can handle." I hold out my empty hand. "Take these."

He looks at it. "Take what?"

"The imaginary scissors to cut the imaginary cord you still try to hold."

Momma Joe laughs, and so do Kiki and Max.

* * *

THE RIDE to the airport was almost silent.

Leaving for college was a big deal, but I always knew I could see any of them at a moment's notice. That won't be the case now.

My favorite movie of all time is *The Wizard of Oz*. When I met Dad for the first time, I felt like Dorthey walking into Emerald City. He filled the entire city and a part of my heart that had always been empty. Then the rest of them filled it even more.

Standing before the entrance to the airport security

check in, I put on a brave face.

As I hug Momma Joe, she whispers, "Be bold but careful. And call me anytime."

"I love you." I hug her extra tightly.

Carly is next. "We're so proud of you."

"I know." I hug her. "Love you Momma C."

Next, I hug Max, the lion to my Dorothy. "Don't you ever forget you're as strong as all the other Steel crew. Be courageous."

"Pft, I know that," he replies as he hugs me tighter.

Kiki is next. "Stow the badass once in a while, Kiki, and let people see your heart."

"They have to earn that," she whispers.

I hug her tighter. "I love you, Katherine."

A tear slides down my face as I look at Dad. "I think I'm going to miss you most of all." *Scarecrow*, I think.

"Don't go." His eyes widen, and I see unshed tears in his them.

I hug him tightly. "Don't ask me to stay when you taught me to fly."

WALKING OUTSIDE of Miami International Airport, the humidity hits me like a hot damp cloth. I smile when I see the palm trees, snap a picture, and send it to the family group chat. After shoving my phone in my crossbody purse, I look around and see a woman in short shorts, a black tank top, and blue hair. Colorful tattoo sleeves cover her toned arms. She's smoking a cigarette and leaning against a white SUV. She flicks it and holds out the sign under her arm that says, *I. Steel*

Smiling, I hurry toward her. "I'm she."

She looks me up and down and busts up laughing. "You have got to be kidding me. Those assholes are going to eat your Barbie ass up."

It pisses me off, but I'm not here to make enemies. As a matter of fact, I'm not here to make friends either. But I will play the game. "They may try, but they won't succeed."

She pushes off the vehicle and blows a puff of smoke in my face. "You wanna bet?"

I ask, "You wanna lose?"

She shakes her head in sarcastic disbelief and moves away from the passenger door. "Get in. We've only got a few hours before we try to salvage this week's shitshow."

I open the back and load my things in, while she sits in the driver's side, impatiently waiting. Well, fuck her. She could have helped.

I climb in. Before I'm even buckled, she peels out and away from the curb.

Once I'm buckled, I turn to her. "So?"

She turns up the radio then pulls a file from between the seat and console, tossing it at me and yelling over the heavy metal music, "Here's the crew."

The first page shows the details of the show that I've already looked up on the website.

Then there is the itinerary. Miami; Las Vegas; Richmond, Virginia; Flint, Michigan; Portland; Austin, Texas; San Francisco; Honolulu, Hawaii; Kansas City, Missouri; Los Angeles; and then to Philadelphia. Eleven stops, two studios in each city, one week at each with appropriate travel time in-between each, as well as time off for the holidays. The earlier stops are hotels. The latter is a mix of homes and hotels.

I open the file and flip through the pages. At the top is a name, and below is information about them.

One by one, I look at their names.

Maze
Grimm
Tags
Axel
Blade
Ranger
Darby
Breaker
Dagger
Neo

"Is this for real?" I laugh.

She pretends she doesn't hear me, and it pisses me off.

I reach up and turn off the stereo. "You don't have to like me, but would it hurt you to answer some fucking questions?"

I see her roll her eyes behind her shades. "First, we aren't friends. You and I, we're rivals, just like they are. They're going up against each other for one hundred Gs, and we're going up against each other for five an episode. One of ours wins, so do we."

"Wasn't aware of that, but I'm good with a paycheck."

"I bet you are, Barbie." She reaches up and turns the stereo back on.

I turn it off. "Listen, Lilith, I'm ten days behind you; you wanna win fair and square, give me more information."

"I don't give a damn how I win." She laughs. "You'll be introduced to them all at dinner, just like I was."

This bitch hasn't a clue that I'm not easily intimidated. Hell, I've dealt with Kat most of my life. This one's a cupcake in comparison.

TEN
DITCH AND DINE
BELLA

When we pull up in front of a beachside motel that looks like it hasn't been renovated in the past two decades, I flip open the folder.

"You sure we're at the right place?" I ask my happy hostess when she kills the engine.

"The guys got us kicked out of the five star two days ago." She opens the door and gets out, and I follow suit. She doesn't move to help me unload my belongings; just lights a cigarette and leans against the driver's side.

I stack everything perfectly on top of my rolling case and begin to head toward the entrance, leaving Smokey the Bitch to finish her cigarette and secretly hoping she chokes on it. Then I look back when I hear the vehicle start.

She rolls down the passenger window and flips me off. "Good luck getting a cab to the hotel at this hour." She peels out.

I stand there, hands full and pissed off.

I pull my phone out and look at the email. Sweating balls, I hit Google and find the hotel fifteen blocks away. Then I hit Uber.

* * *

FORTY MINUTES LATER, sweat-drenched, I walk into the Sand Beach Resort. Beyond the fountain and behind a wall of glass, I spot Bitchzilla and a bunch of inked men sitting at the hotel bar.

I drop my bags at the desk, and a woman looks me over, scrunching her nose up a little. "Can I help you?"

"Isabella Steel, and I'll be right back for my room key. Hold my bags please."

I stomp through the lobby, fuming, through the opening in the glass wall and straight up to her. I tap her on the shoulder, and she whips around.

She immediately laughs in my face until I step into her space.

"You better check yourself, Barbie."

I look up as I close the gap between us, my tits pressing against hers. "You just fucked up with me."

She steps forward. I hold my stance. "You best—"

"You think you, your bad attitude, and bad dye job intimidate me? You're fucking wrong. I'm a grown-ass woman, not some little bitch you can bully on the playground because your daddy didn't pay enough attention to you. You've been warned."

I swing around and begin to walk back to the reception desk when I feel a hand shove me from behind.

As I fall, I reach for the table, knowing damn well I'm going to bust my face on it. Instead, an arm snakes around my waist and catches me.

I try to wiggle my way out, but the bulging arm tightens, and then I'm lifted off the ground and carried past the desk, out the back door, and toward the ocean.

"Let go of me now, or so help me God, I will bust your nuts with my damn heel."

A dark chuckle reverberates against my back as the man hastens his steps.

I try to turn, but he moves so I can't see him. Then I try to kick, but he turns me and heaves me over his shoulder.

"Let me down!"

When I see water underneath me, I realize this lunatic is walking into the ocean.

"I said …" I begin as he grips my waist and pulls me down until I am knee-deep in the water.

When I look up, I gasp when he smiles.

Natural instinct kicks in, and I slap him across the face.

He narrows his eyes. "Hey, sweet treat. Did you miss me?"

Tags

WHEN I SAW her storming into the bar, I swore to God I was seeing things, and I haven't had a drop of alcohol in over a year, done any type of drug in over four. When I saw her go up against Mara, heard her voice, and heard the sass it carried, I was pretty sure the sweat-drenched, little wannabe badass wasn't a doppelganger of the girl I fucked at my buddy's shop just days ago.

It wasn't until I saw that ass bent over and falling that I knew without a doubt it was.

This isn't good.

She reaches up to slap me again, but I catch her hand this time. When she starts to yank away, pull her against me, hard.

"No swimming or you fuck up the gift."

"The gift!" She raises her knee and gets me where she intended. I hold back every ounce of pain that comes with a knee to the nuts and smile at her. "You tagged me!"

"My bad."

"Your bad?" She's pissed. She's really fucking pissed. "And you're married!"

Impulse control is a real issue with me, but I hold in the explanation when I realize this is going to work in my favor. I piss her off, she stays away. I'm gonna *really* need her to stay away.

"You smug bastard," she sneers.

"You wanna pop off some bullshit, you do it when this is done. This is work, sweets, not pleasure."

"Fuck you," she spits.

"Told you already; six to nine months, then we chat."

"We aren't chatting about shit!"

"Glad we agree. But I will do you a solid and give you a heads-up."

She splashes past me. "Go fuck yourself."

"Mara is Gorgon's daughter."

"Who the hell is Mara?" She doesn't slow down; she keeps on going.

"The chick with the bad attitude and dye job."

She looks back. "So what?"

"She's also a real bitch, not a sweet, little treat who just graduated college."

"I don't give a damn."

"You want this job, I suggest you chill." I grab her bicep and stop her. "You wanna keep it, forget you and I ever met."

She pulls her arm away. "That won't be hard to do."

I can't help laughing as I follow behind her, eyes on her ass. "You and I both know that's not true."

She glares at me from over her shoulder. "I fucked you in a tattoo shop; you were forgotten once I came."

As much as I need to focus on winning this show, my inability to control myself comes out in full force. "Which time?"

When she turns on me quickly, I'm taken aback.

"The *last* time," she snarls then pushes me.

I lose my footing, my ass hits the water, and a wave washes over me.

When I come up, there are nine assholes standing on the beach. The biggest one high-fives Bella then offers her his arm. She takes it, and then I watch them walk inside ... together.

Fucking Neo.

I ball my fists at my sides but smile as I walk past all the jackasses on the beach who watched the little show.

Maze, the oldest of the contestants, turns and grabs my shoulder as he walks beside me. "So, you met the new producer?"

"Sure did, Maze."

"Doesn't look like she likes you any more than the last one did."

I shrug his arm off me, and he laughs.

"If you weren't a decent artist, they'd probably boot your ass. Thank the universe that you're the second best here."

I laugh at him. "Who exactly is the universe?"

He shrugs. "What came first—the chicken or the egg?"

"Which one's female?"

"Huh?" He's confused.

"The female always comes first."

* * *

Bella

"YOU'RE NOT NORMALLY my type but want a real man to fuck that cunt good, then look no further."

There are men who can say the filthiest things in the world and still make you feel sexy, and then there are men who utter the exact same words and leave you feeling like you haven't showered in a month and smell like ass.

Neo is the latter. He's also one-third of the reason I'm trying to scald my skin.

Standing under a hot stream of water in the shower, I scrub my body, ridding it of the filth I just unhooked my arm from, the sweat from my three-mile walk in the ninety-eight degree Miami heat, and the nasty I feel because ... his touch sent my body into a tizzy.

He's so fucking hot and so fucking married.

Tags. His name is Tags. Or, at least that's what they called him.

After I have scrubbed my body and left the ache between my legs—caused by him—unattended, I wrap myself in the plush white hotel towel and walk out into the suite to dress and meet everyone for dinner.

The suite is not mine alone. I'm sharing it with ... her.

I look around for my bags, but they are nowhere to be found, and the balcony door is open.

That bitch probably put my shit outside.

Tightening the towel, I walk out and see my makeup bag and its content scattered on the balcony's tiled floor.

I look over the railing and see my undergarments, clothes ... and my suitcase floating around the resort's pool and lazy river.

"Fucking bitch!" I snarl as I turn around and see her smiling with her teeth bared as she closes the balcony door and locks it. "Open this door now, Mara."

She flips me off then turns, giving me her back as she walks toward the main door.

I beat on the glass. "Open the fucking door!"

When she walks out the door, I scream, "You cu—"

A loud laugh cuts off the rest of the vulgarity ready to fly out of my mouth, a word I have never had to use.

I quickly look left.

He has a towel wrapped low on his waist.

"We could have saved water and showered together."

"I'd rather swim in shit, *Tags*." I say his name like a taunting teen would.

"All right then." He lifts one of his bulging shoulders. "I guess you're on your own."

"Better than being on you," I snip back.

When he grins, I immediately regret my choice of words.

He lifts his chin. "Yeah right."

I lean over the edge of the balcony. Three floors. I can do this. If things go bad, I can leap and will land in the pool, unscathed, and grab my clothes.

"Bad idea, little badass."

I glare over at him. "Go away."

Out of my peripheral, I see him walk inside his room. *Thank God.*

As quick as he goes in, he comes back out. He tosses something at me. It hits me in the face, and I let it drop to the floor. "Put that on and sit your ass still for a minute. I'll open your door from the inside."

"Oh, and how are you going to get in?" I ask, propping a hand on my hip.

He looks down, and I realize I've had a Janet Jackson and the nip slip incident. "You're gonna make winning this as hard as you're making my dick, sweets."

"How about you grow up and focus on your wife?"

"She hasn't been really receptive for the past two years and nine months, sweets."

"I wonder why with a man like you."

He scrubs his hand over his face, sighs, and then shakes his head. "I'm just gonna put it out there that your apology is already accepted."

"You're a piece of work, you know."

He gives me a blinding smiling. His eyes even sparkle.

Damn his hotness.

"I'm glad you noticed."

Before I have the chance to yell at him, he's already gone.

I do not want his help, I think as I lean over the railing again.

Less than a minute, maybe even a moment later, the door to the balcony slides open. I look back and see him, Tags, standing behind me in ball shorts and a black tank top. I bite back a *thank you*, because I don't want to be nice, and step toward the doorway that he's filling.

I'm about to tell him to get the hell out of the way when I see his eyes searching, seeking, and then, in a blink, it's gone.

He sighs. "You're a producer."

"You're in my way."

"Do you have any fucking idea how hard this is gonna be for you and me?"

"Only because you're making it so." I scowl.

He leans in and swallows hard. I like the way his Adam's apple ...

No, fuck no.

His hot breath caresses my face as he says, "Show me what I see in you is real, show me you're strong, and I'll show you I'm stronger."

"You're a married man."

"It's complicated."

"Leave me alone." I hear the plea in my voice, meant to be masked.

"I already know that's impossible." He grips my hips and pulls me toward him.

"Please don't," I nearly beg as he leans in, his lips centimeters from mine.

But he does.

* * *

WHEN I WALK OUTSIDE and onto the hotel restaurant's patio where a family-style dinner is already being served to a table of two dozen people—the cast and what I assume is the crew—I do so with pride, even knowing how absolutely ridiculous I look.

The first person I see is Tags. He leans back in his chair and covers his smile.

"Oh damn," one of the guys fists his hand and holds it in front of his mouth.

I search the table until I see David Gorgon, the executive producer. Then, holding my head high while trying to walk in the six-inch pleather boots that are two sizes too big for me, I ignore the annoyance in his eyes.

When he looks left to Mara, his daughter, he glares at her.

She rolls her eyes flippantly and sits back.

I reach out my hand. "Mr. Gorgon, I'm Isabella Steel, and I want to thank you for the opportunity."

"Ass-kisser," Mara mumbles.

Ignoring his daughter, David stands and shakes my hand. "It's a pleasure to meet you." He keeps his eyes on mine, telling me he's a gentleman, since he's not staring at my tits popping out of the leather bustier that I tried to cover with the tank top that Tags had thrown at me that I'm now wearing as a dress.

"Have a seat. You missed appetizers, but dinner is ready."

"Wardrobe malfunction." I smile, and he looks at his daughter.

She shrugs.

There are a few chairs open, but the one next to her, well, it's calling my name.

"You've got to be kidding me."

I ignore her sneer and sit next to her.

The girl on the other side smiles. "Hi, I'm Maxine, Mr. Gorgon's—"

"Whore," Mara mumbles under her breath.

I quickly look at David, who either didn't hear her or is ignoring her. Then I look back at Maxine. "I'm Isabella."

"Nice to meet you."

Mara leans forward. "How about you two share a room?"

"Um ..." Maxine says, looking at David

He stands up. "Mara, a word."

"No."

When he leans down and whispers in her ear, she stands up, nearly toppling her chair over. I catch it and right it before it hits the floor.

ELEVEN
INTRODUCTIONS
TAGS

She looks sexy, edible, fuckable, and every other -able you can think of. I get it; her clothes were all soaked when I fished them out of the pool and set them at her doorstep. She had no choice but to play the little temptress.

The problem is that every other fucker in here is thinking the same shit as I am, and it pisses me off.

Pushing past pissed and trying to act a little more civilized, I get a conversation going ... that's not just in my head. "While we wait for those two to return, why don't we all introduce ourselves to our newest producer?"

"Why?" Neo huffs. "She won't be here long."

"I think she just proved she will be," I say in the least aggressive way I can.

"The last one left crying. This one's gonna piss Mayhem off one more time and end up leaving in a body bag."

My fists ball at my sides. "Not likely."

"She's the only one of us without a record; she'd get away with it, too." Dagger shrugs.

I look at Bella, whose eyes widen for a split-second then relax again.

"I'll start," Maze, the oldest of us, says. "Name's Maze. The crime is fleeing from the police, a misdemeanor. Then evading, a felony."

"Grimm, grave robbing."

"Blade, armed robbery."

"Let me guess; with a knife?" Isabella asks.

He smiles and nods.

"Axel, B&E."

"Ranger, drunk and disorderly."

"Darby, DUI."

"Breaker, also B&E."

"Dagger, felony possession."

"Neo, possession and unlawfully dealing with a minor." He narrows his eyes at me.

I look at Bella and roll out my laundry list, "Tags, started with shoplifting, vandalism, breaking and entering, assault, and the last one was vandalism again."

"A few times," Neo mumbles.

I look away from him and back at her. "Yeah, a few times."

She's unreadable. Then she grabs the glass of water in front of her, takes a drink, and sits back. "Cool. So, aside from being artists and felons, what else is there to know about you?"

"How about you tell us about you?" Neo says, looking her over.

"All right. I'm not a tattoo artist but grew up in a shop. My family ran one."

"Cupcake shop?" Axel asks.

"Tattoo shop. I've just completed my masters degree

and am happy to be here despite the unwelcome reception. But I'm going to chalk it up to a hazing of sorts and move on."

"Where you from?" Maze asks.

"New Jersey."

"Just across the river from a few of us." He smiles, and she nods.

"You get the job because of your family or the same way Maxine got hers?" Blade asks her.

"My education," she answers as she reaches for the bowl of green beans.

"Uh-huh." Neo laughs.

She nudges Maxine, who's looking down at her empty plate sullenly. "Beans?"

She shakes her head.

"Allergic?"

Again, she shakes her head.

Bella spoons some out on her plate. "You have to eat something."

"So, you have no problem working with a bunch of felons?" Maze asks her.

"I treat people the way they treat me." She passes the beans to him. "If I'm assigned you and you run, I'll catch you quicker than the cops."

He laughs, and so do some of the others.

When David returns, Mara's not with him.

Holding his tie to his shirt, he sits and gives Maxine a wink. I look at Bella and see her nudge Maxine, who's now smiling.

"All right, tomorrow we're back at Mayhem. Ten a.m. sharp. No fucking excuses. No bullshit. We have a budget to stick to. We go over budget, we do double eliminations to make up for it. We're doing mothers and daughters. I need good footage, not wasted hours, you all hear me?"

We nod, and not because we're little bitches, but because we all need a fucking paycheck.

"Still no elimination in the plans for week one, unless we can't get shit. You're on camera, be you. But remember, we're hoping this gets picked up by a major network."

He looks at Bella. "Sorry about Mara."

"She and I will be fine," Bella states matter-of-factly.

"Any ideas, changes, directions you think we should take?" he asks her.

"I'd like to reserve judgment until I actually see what works and what else doesn't."

"You said *what else*; clearly you have an issue with something." David leans forward.

"The name, *Fifty Shades of Ink*." She throws her thumb over her shoulder. "None of these guys look like how any of us picture Christian."

"It's a play on words."

"It's misguiding the audience; breaking trust before it's even established," she counters.

"Sex sells."

She nods. "I agree. You picked a hot cast."

"Hell yes, they did." Blade laughs.

She ignores him and continues, "But they're not pretty boys."

Dagger, the one who looks like a toddler got ahold of a Ken doll and a Sharpie, huffs, "Some of us are very pretty."

"I'm all man. I'll be glad to prove it," Neo taunts.

She points to him without looking. "Some seemingly overcompensate."

"Give me two minutes, and I'll prove you wrong," he retorts.

She does look at him now. “You just proved me right. Two minutes isn’t worth my time.”

The table erupts in *ooo*’s and laughter.

She looks back at David. “Many women want to tame the bad boy, and some just want to experience the fantasy, the forbidden. You have a table full of ex-cons.”

Several mumble under their breaths, but she doesn’t stop.

“All who I’m sure have stories of how they rose up and ended up here. Give your audience something to cheer for.”

“Go on,” David encourages her.

“I agree that sex sells, but so does rooting for the underdog. It gives us all hope.”

“Give me a name,” he says while picking up his drink.

“I haven’t really thought it through.”

I watch as he considers what she has to say. Then, a split-second later, the look is gone.

“We’ll stick with *Fifty Shades of Ink*.”

I look around the table and see a divide. The majority like her idea.

Damn, sweet treat, just ... damn.

After dinner, David stands. “Let’s all get a good night’s sleep so we can bring our A game tomorrow.”

I watch as Bella makes it a point to say goodnight to everyone. Doesn’t mean I like it, but I watch it, trying to figure out her tells. To see how she shakes each hand, her body language, her facial expressions, and the way she leaves the conversation.

When she gets to me, she looks up, her smile as bright as it was with the others. “So, you’re married and a felon?”

“Makes you want to bring me right home and meet the folks, doesn’t it?”

She frowns, turns, and walks away.

And I have to let her.

* * *

I'M NOT A STALKER. I laugh at the thought as I eavesdrop on the conversation next door. It's not like I climbed across the eighteen-inch gap between the balconies, pressed my body against the wall so I wasn't seen, or put my ear to the glass to overhear what is going on. Their door's cracked ... or I would have.

Mara is moving her things to another room, at David's insistence. She's pissed that she has to move. I'm annoyed that Isabella offered to do so. She's now waiting for Isabella to give her the boots, fishnets, and leather, laced-up bodysuit Bella had to wear because of Mara's bullshit.

"Don't make me take it off you," Mara snaps at her.

"You may be six inches taller than me and spend a hell of a lot more time at the gym than I do, but look at me, Mara, look at me and realize what oozes from me. It isn't fear; it's determination. So you fucking wait until my shit's dry or you're gonna have your hands full."

"You think I won't?"

"You wanna be on camera tomorrow with a split lip and a couple of black eyes, bring it."

I hear feet rustling and jump up, ready to jump in.

"You just fucking pushed me!" Mara screams.

"Get in my face again and you'll get worse, bitch."

Aw fuck.

"Did you just call me a bitch!"

"You've certainly earned it and are one step away from cunt, so if you're offended, Mayhem—"

"What did you just call me?"

Here we fucking go.

Bella laughs. "Cunt offends you so much, don't act like one."

One foot on the railing, the other on a chair, I'm ready to pounce.

"Mayhem. Who told you my street name?"

"Overheard it." I hear more rustling. "Now there's your fucking leather. Get the hell out."

"Nice tits. Your daddy buy them for you?" Mara sneers.

"Tits this nice can't be bought. Now get the fuck out of my room."

"Neo may have put his dick in you, but you'll never win his heart."

"I wouldn't fuck him with your," she pauses, "cunt."

When I hear the door slam, I hop back onto the balcony floor.

David was dead wrong to put Mara in the same room with anyone after the bullshit she pulled on the last chick—a hairpulling, cat scratching, chick fight that all the guys enjoyed way too fucking much ... until they realized it's the reason we're not having three days here in Miami without work before we move on to our next location—Las Vegas. All the guys are psyched about the move.

"Hey, Dad." Pause. "No, I'm good." Pause. "I didn't call because I was busy. I sent a picture in the group chat at the airport and at the hotel." Pause. "No, it's good. It'll be a challenge." Pause. "Oh my God, really?" She laughs. "It's my first day. First five hours, actually. If it wasn't a challenge, I'd be bored." Pause. "I'm good, Dad, really," she huffs. "But nothing, I don't need you here." Pause. "I'm taking care of it. And no, I'm not giving you a name." Pause. "I'm going to say I love you now, because I feel I'm real close to hanging up on you." Pause, and then she laughs. "Well, knock it off then. I'm good; better than good." Pause. "Do you not remember I survived six years in New York City." Pause. "Love you, too, Daddy."

That phrase, Daddy, shouldn't rub me the wrong way, but it does.

"Tell everyone I said hi, and I love them. Bye."

I find myself questioning, *Who is everyone?*

When she walks out and looks at me, hand on her hip, in *my* tee-shirt and a pair of PJ shorts, she asks, "Why don't you worry more about your wife and less about who *everyone* is?" I realize I asked the question out loud.

I sit back in the chair, kick my feet up on the railing, and grab my smokes off the table beside me.

"Well?"

I smirk then light a smoke, take a drag, lean my head back on the chair, and blow the smoke in the air. "Just curious about the girl whose pussy I crave."

"You seriously had no right to kiss me, and you will not do it again. Ever."

I pull my feet down and sit up. "Because I'm married, or a felon?"

She opens her mouth then shuts it twice before saying, "I don't care what you've done in your past, but being married—"

"That's in my past, too." I snuff out the cigarette and stand.

"You're presently married."

"But I don't want to be." I cross the floor and step on the chair.

She holds her hand up. "Stop."

"What if I don't want to do that either?"

When I step on the chair and put one foot on the ledge, she steps back.

"Get away from me."

"Your mouth says no; your nipples are a go." I step on the ledge.

"Go," she says, "meaning *go away*."

Standing, both feet on the ledge, she covers her eyes. "If you fall—"

"We'll fall together." I step across then jump down.

Spreading her fingers, she looks through them at me.

"This is not a good idea." I walk toward her. "I say six to nine months, and here you are. I say you need to forget we met, and you're in the next room. Your lips begged to be kissed, and I couldn't tell you no—"

"They didn't!" Her back is now against the glass. "You need to leave."

"Give me one good reason why."

"You. Are. Married." She pushes at my chest.

I don't move; I simply tell her the truth. "I'm trying to get divorced."

She attempts to step back again, right into the glass.

I laugh. "Can't even think when I'm around."

"It's called playing defense, you conceited ass, because you can't keep your hands off me."

Placing my hands on the glass on each side of her head, I lean in. "See that? You feel me and I'm not even touching you ... yet."

"I'm not interested in fucking up my job or a married man."

"I'm trying to get divorced."

She slides under my arm. "Look, Tags, you and I are going to have to work together, even though I think you're a complete and total ass for doing this shit to me." She points to her back. “It can be fixed. But you can’t fix the fact that you cheated on a woman you made a promise to.” She motioned between us. “This isn’t happening.”

“It did happen. It’s still happening.”

When my phone vibrates in my pocket, I realize it’s that time. I can’t ignore it without suffering the mental terrorism inflicted by an unanswered call from thirty-five inches of crazy.

I turn around, putting my back to Bella, pull out my phone, and answer with, “What color’s the sky?”

“Pink and yellow.”

“Pink and yellow, huh?”

“What color’s yours?” she asks.

I look up. “Just so happens to be the same. You know why that is, Luna?”

“Same sky.”

“Same sky,” I agree.

“Same sun?”

“Same sun.”

“And what about the moon?” she asks.

“You’re in charge of the moon, Luna. You tell me.”

“The moon’s tired.”

I laugh. “Then the moon should go to sleep.”

“You going to sleep?”

“I sure am.”

“Love you, Daddy.”

“Love you, too, Luna. Give the old lady a hug goodnight.”

She giggles. God, I love her laugh.

“Face phone in the morning?”

“Every morning till I see you again.”

“I get a puppy when we win,” she whispers.

"Yeah, baby girl, you get a puppy when we win. Love you, Luna."

"Love you, Daddy."

I wait until she hangs up then turn around in time to stop Bella from closing the door behind her.

"Now, where were we?" I ask.

"I was about to shut the door and lock it, but I have a better idea."

"Yeah?"

She takes my hands and walks me into her room.

"I like where this is leading. I like it a lot, sweets."

Dropping one of my hands, she turns and continues walking.

My eyes are on her ass, willing to go wherever she leads me, until she opens the door leading to the hallway.

"You're a married man, and I'm going to assume that call was your daughter. You're leaving through a door, not putting your life in—"

I pull her back in the room and shut the door.

She shoves me, and I get that she's pissed.

"Not a good idea to be seen leaving your room. What would the neighbors think?"

"They'd think I was serious about my job, and not a cheating whore."

I see tears. I hate tears. Especially tears in the eyes of a female. Be it in sadness, pain, or about to flip shit, I hate them.

I hold my hands up and step back. "Okay."

"Okay? Okay!" She steps forward and pushes me.

I nod. "Okay."

She walks back to the door and opens it. "Now go."

"Sweets ..." I begin.

"Don't call me that!"

"Fuck." I hurry to the door, shut it, pick her up, and then set her on the bed.

"Don't you—"

"I'm trusting you."

"I wouldn't if I were you." She scurries back.

"I'm trusting you, and I expect—"

"Get OUT!"

"Mara, she's my wife."

TWELVE
REAL TALK
BELLA

If ever there was a time that I wanted my daddy, it was right now. I feel sick to my stomach and truly fearful for probably the first time in my life.

Mara, aka Mayhem, the executive producer's daughter, is the wife of the man I fucked. The man who tagged me.

When he sits on the edge of the hotel bed, all I can do is look at him.

"She isn't going to try to hurt you or any shit like that because you and I are fucking."

"No? Because, before she even knew I fucked her husband, she dumped me off a few miles away from here."

"It's a long story."

"I don't want to hear it." I shake my head back and forth.

He fills in the blanks. "But you need to."

"I still don't want to hear it."

"Neo and I met in juvy. He was in for drugs. I was in for"—he smirks, and I want to kick him—"vandalism. When we got out, I didn't have a home to go back to, and he didn't have one he wanted to return to, so we became family."

My skin crawls at the thought of that.

"We joined a gang. We met Mayhem at a rave. We were all fucked up; had a threesome. The next morning, we wake up in a fat pad, and Neo decided she was his. A few months later, she's pregnant and it was too late to do anything about it. Neo ditched her, because the baby came out my color and not his. He took off. She insisted I marry her. A few months later, she was gone, and Luna, my daughter, and I were on our own."

I want to scream, run, cry, hide ... kick his ass, hug him, kick my own ass for wanting to hug him, but I say nothing.

"Mara's been in and out of rehab for the past couple years. She hasn't seen Luna since she left. She's avoided being served. I hired a PI and found out about her father."

"And now you know he has money and—"

"I don't give a damn about money; I give a damn about my girl. I want a divorce so we can move on."

We?

"Luna and I," he answers my unspoken question. Then he pulls out his phone and turns it. The screensaver is of him and a little girl. "She just started asking about her mom this year—since she started preschool. Paula said—"

"Who's Paula?" I'm holding his phone that I didn't even realize I'd taken, scrolling through pictures. She's beautiful.

"An older woman who took me, a nineteen-year-old, homeless gangbanger with an infant, into her home on a hunch. She took care of that baby when I turned myself in for my past mistakes, told me to learn a trade while I was in jail for a year, and didn't ask for shit in return. A woman who had a job lined up for me when I was released from jail. A woman who gave me hope. I owe her for helping me remember why I need to be the best man, the best father I can be."

The softness in his voice makes me look up.

"I'm going to pay her back for what she has given us." His eyes search mine, and then he stands up off the bed. "She lost her two kids to gang violence yet still believes there's good in the world. I'm gonna prove to her she's right."

I watch him pace back and forth at the end of my bed, then he stops and pins me with an intense stare before smiling. "And I'm gonna prove to you that what I put on your back was the truth because, Isabella Steel, the moment I saw you, I knew it to be true. That kind of connection doesn't happen every day—never in my lifetime—and I know damn well you feel the same."

I open my mouth to deny the statement, but nothing comes out. I consider the possibility that the reason I'm unable to reply is that I know what I would say isn't the truth. But the things he's saying about us aren't real, are they? I mean, they sound real, feel real, and I want to kick my own ass because I want them to be real, but ... really?

I don't know why I close my eyes—possibly in hopes to see the truth—but all I see is the dozen or so happy couples I've been surrounded by most of my life. None of them had a well-executed plan on how to fall in love, none of them in the best places in their lives; it just happened.

Like this is, a voice inside of me whispers.

But he crossed a line. I should be so pissed at him.

Yet here you are.

When I open my eyes, I know he sees me—my wants, my desires, my confusion, the incredible respect I already have for him, or how astoundingly smitten I am with him.

"I'd rather be inside you than on the other side of that wall. I'll wait for you to accept it. But, for every night I'm wishing I was inside of you, you'll get two nights where you'll beg for me." He exits the room the way he came in, and I fight the urge to go after him.

It's easy to do, because I'm not sure if I want to tell him how delusional he is ... and possibly me, too, or do what feels good—him.

Sleep doesn't come easy as I lie here, thinking about the little girl, Luna, and the similarities between her and me. No, my mom didn't leave me in the same way that Luna was left, but she was left just the same. Her father wasn't forbidden then court-ordered to stay away from her, but the way he spoke of her and the ... nauseating similarities between him and my father and uncles is apparent.

He would prove her right. He wanted better for his girl. And the statement about Neo: *we became family ...*

Fuck!

I sigh as I roll over onto my stomach and bury my head in the pillows that smell like *her*.

I jump up and pull the blankets off the bed, dragging them to the door so that maid service would take them away. Then I walk over to the glass doors to shut them and see my phone sitting on the table. When I walk out, the smell of cigarette smoke mixed with the smell of the Atlantic Ocean lingers in the humid, evening air.

I look over as he looks up. In the moonlight, I can still see his eyes. The initial confusion morphs into lust.

"I forgot my phone." I walk over and grab for it as he stands, butts out his cigarette, and then walks over to the railing.

"I'm sorry you haven't had it easy."

"I'm not," he says with conviction.

My hand still on the phone, I lift my chin. "How does a man like David, with all the resources he has at his disposal, allow his daughter—"

"He doesn't know about me or Luna."

"Impossible."

"I know for sure he doesn't know about Luna."

"Why would you keep her away from her family?"

He lifts a shoulder.

I pick up my phone and start to walk back in then stop. "If he's a good man, it isn't fair to either of them, Tags, or whatever your name is."

"Carter. And tell me, Isabella, what kind of father allows his teenage daughter to live the life she has? If he gave a fuck, she wouldn't have been eighteen with a million-dollar penthouse in New York City."

"I know nothing about her, except she's a bitch who has a beautiful little girl she has nothing to do with."

"So many people think they need to force a relationship between kids and their biological family, thinking any type of relationship with them is beneficial. That's like saying if you're in Flint and have nothing to drink but poisonous water, it's better to do that than die of thirst. I'm not of the mindset that biology means shit. She has a mother figure—better one than I was birthed from—and she has me."

"But ..." I begin then stop because *but nothing*. He's right.

"But?"

I shake my head.

"But what?"

"Goodnight, Carter."

"People I like a hell of a lot less than the woman who gave me that name call me Tags, Isabella. I'd prefer that."

I turn back and look at him. "Was *she*," meaning Mara, "one of them?"

He nods.

"Goodnight, John Boy."

He laughs as I walk back into my room and close the door behind me.

After plugging my phone into the charging station, I go brush my teeth. When I walk out, I expect to see him standing in my room.

He's not.

I walk over to lock the door that I had consciously left unlocked then decide against it. I like him. I like the way he looks at me. I like the way he talks to me. I like the way he feels inside of me. And although I will never admit it and will get the damn thing fixed, I like that he likes me enough to "tag" me. And yes, that all pisses me off.

When I lie down and smell her perfume again, I'm further irritated.

After stripping the bed, I open the door to the balcony and peek out.

When my eyes meet his, they narrow.

"Can't sleep?"

"The room smells like bad mom."

He smirks and shakes his head. "Mine smells like me."

"How did you get a single room?"

"I'm one hell of a negotiator and an even better artist." He walks over to the balcony and leans forward. "Do you trust me, sweets?"

Not yet, I think. Quickly, I say, "I'm not fucking you."

His eyes dance in amusement as he replies, "That's good, because you denied me, so all you'll get, if you're lucky, is a big spoon."

I look at him then over the edge and back up at him.

"It's eighteen inches, only a little bit bigger than my dick, and you didn't flinch at that."

I step back and scowl at him. "I'm still mad at you about the tattoo."

"Impulse control."

"Shitty excuse."

"The real one makes you act all kinds of crazy."

She is mine, I wonder if that's what he means.

"I've dealt with crazy, Isabella, and I definitely prefer your brand over that of an abusive mother and ex—"

"Oh my God, shut up please."

He smiles, knowing he's gotten under my skin. "Wait until I show you all the scars from my days in the Marines."

"You were in the military?"

He laughs as he shakes his head. "I was living in abandoned warehouses by the river, fighting a little war called survival." He stops when I step onto the chair.

"The tattoo shop was a fluke. You gained my respect because of your daughter and the fact you're not cheating on your wife. Well, not really."

"Never wanted to be that man, Isabella. My word was all I had to offer back then. It's the most important thing I have to offer now and forever."

Looking down, my stomach does summersaults, and not just because I hate heights but because he is *so* hot. "You don't get my trust because of your sad story. We all have one of those."

"I can't wait to lick away all your pain."

I fight back a smile. "This is me seeing if I can actually trust you."

He smirks and looks down. "Let's hope I don't drop you. You'd survive that, and I'm sure you're the kind of girl who would never forget it."

I laugh nervously. "How the hell would I survive it?"

"Because, Isabella Steel, if I'm asking you to trust me, it means I will do anything to make sure you don't question it, and it would take a hell of a lot longer than I plan to take gaining your trust when we're lying in hospital beds."

"We?" I huff.

"Simple law of gravity. I weigh more. When I jump after you, I'd hit the ground first and cushion your fall."

I give him the same look I have gotten all my life when being taught something important. "That's not true; free falling objects fall at the same rate of acceleration."

"My bad. That wasn't covered in the GED classes I took."

"I'm trusting you."

"I'll make sure you never regret it."

I nod, take a deep breath, and then I jump.

"Oh my God!" I laugh as my heart beats wildly inside my chest. "Feel this." I take his hand and hold it to my chest. "Do you feel that?" I look up at him as I try to control my heartbeat.

His eyes are black, and I have never wanted to run into the dark more than I do right now.

"A little lower and to the left, and I'd be feeling a hell of a lot more."

My nipples tighten immediately, and everything inside of me begins to pulse.

"Kiss me." My voice is husky, unrecognizable even to me.

"I'm gonna do a hell of a lot more than kiss you, Isabella Steel." Pulling me tightly against his insanely hot, hard, inked body, he wraps his arms around me and lifts me up so we are eye to eye. "I'm gonna lick all your past pains away and have you looking forward to a tomorrow full of"—when he stops, I smile, waiting for something profound—"palm trees and a pleasant breeze."

Well, it wasn't all that profound, but it works.

When his lips scorch mine, I realize I don't give a damn if this man isn't a poet, I don't give a damn that he's married —sort of—and I don't give a damn that he feels like home, knowing it's because he looks and acts like a lot of those from home ...

"What?" he asks, laying me on a bed that smells just like him.

"Don't ask." I sit back up, grab his face, and kiss him ... hard.

When he moves his fingers from my "heartbeat" and finds his way between my legs, I cry out when he pushes two inside me and releases a guttural growl.

Bowing his head, he pushes his tee-shirt that I'm wearing to the side and sucks my nipple into his mouth, biting down on it. My head falls back as pulsing changes to thrumping.

Is thrumping even a thing? I ask myself as he pushes me back, thrusting fingers in a frenzy as he nearly eats my tit ... one then the other.

When he rips my pajama shorts down and kisses his way down my belly, I thrust my hips upward. He stalls, and I look down.

"What?" I gasp.

"How badly do you want me to eat your pussy right now, sweet treat?" The look in his eyes is menacing, taunting. He's daring me to answer with the truth.

I manage to keep my voice almost level when I answer, "I could take it or leave it."

He smiles almost sadistically as he pulls my legs apart and begins to lick me roughly while fucking me with his fingers.

Lips, tongue, teeth ... "Oh God!"

I reach between my legs and fist his hair, grinding against his face with no shame.

He pulls his fingers out of me.

"What?"

With the back of his hand, he wipes remnants of my "almost pleasure" from his lips. "How fucking bad, sweets?"

I narrow my eyes. "I'm good."

Laughing, he stands, the head of his cock fully visible, peeking out from under his waistband.

I push up on my elbows, eyeballing his perfection. "And how are you doing?"

He squeezes his eyes shut and, through clenched teeth, replies, "Big spoon."

When he starts to turn away from me, I scurry to the end of the bed like a hungry little whore and grab the waistband of his shorts, pulling him back. As he turns toward me, with his fists balled at his sides, I look at his body, taking in the art. His broad, sexy chest is heaving, his Adam's apple bobs, his jaw is tense, and when my eyes meet his, I know he's just as high on lust as I am.

"After what you did to my back, I shouldn't want to do this as badly as I do."

"But you can't control it, can you?" He wraps his hand around my neck firmly but gently then bends down and kisses my lips before whispering against them, "Really fucking big, really fucking hard spoon." He pushes me back then falls beside me face-first on the bed.

"You're kidding me, right?" I half-laugh, half-pout.

"My word." He rolls onto his side and sighs out, "My fucking word."

I reach up and touch his lips, running my fingers over them and back again. He gives me a less steamy ... sweeter smile.

"You have really pretty lips."

"Yeah?" he asks.

I nod as I trace them. "Very kissable."

"You have an advantage there." His lips curl up in the corners. "Two sets, equally as sexy."

I hold in the schoolgirl giggle I'm afraid will erupt.

I rub my thumb over his eyebrow and down, gently making his eye close then the next. "Telling eyes, too."

"Only to those I want to know."

"To know what?" I whisper.

"Everything," he whispers back.

I run my hands down his nose where the thin silver hoop hangs, his lips, his chin, his neck, between the two women tattooed on his neck. "Who are they?"

He takes my hand and holds it, placing my fingers against his lips. "Not yet, Isabella Steel. Not yet." He lightly pushes me to my back. "Be the little spoon and sleep before I fork the hell out of you."

THIRTEEN
BREAKFAST
TAGS

Sleeping next to the sweetest smelling, tastiest little thing I've ever had the pleasure of making a meal out of was heaven. Sliding out of bed away from her is hell. But I have to stick to the plan: get up, work out, and chat with Luna and Paula as I fuel up.

I look back at her as she sleeps like a fucking baby. Then I open the door to the room and see the elevator opening across the way.

Perfect timing.

I whisper, "Good morning," to the room service staff and slip him a twenty. "I'll take it from here."

He nods, looking at me like everyone does—with nervousness, intimidated, sometimes scared as hell. Not gonna say I don't like it, because I do.

I wheel the cart in and put it beside the bed, looking at her one last time before leaving.

Leaving a hotel room with a sleeping woman isn't an oddity but leaving one like her is.

Smiling to myself, I think about how much I like the fact that she's not intimidated at all.

Paula always told me, if they don't look beyond the ink, they don't deserve to see me. Then, when I decided to start lifting to release my anger, frustration, and all the shit that outweighed me, she laughed and said, "You're gonna get the ones who want the arm candy."

She was right. Every woman with some sort of point to prove wants to date me. After Luna got to the point where she was sleeping through the night, I indulged.

Sisco called them all Beverlys, because they all looked like they wanted to be from Beverly Hills, flashing around cash like they just sucked it out of Daddy's wallet or some big daddy's dick. It never bothered me that I didn't have a fat wallet. Apparently, a fat cock is harder to find than a man with money in Manhattan. Didn't hurt my pride one bit because, when they were on their backs or on all fours ... I was the only daddy they were thinking of.

Just like everything else that made me feel good, it became an addiction. Then, when Luna started asking questions about everything under the sun, she became more real to me. That was when it wasn't about making sure she survived anymore; it was about making sure she could grow up proud, and I sure as fuck wasn't proud of how I'd been living.

Three women in three years offered to take care of me and my daughter, not one had anything to offer either of us that would have been lasting. Sure, I could have made it last —a good dick and a man who knew his word was more valuable than any trust fund was something they all said they wanted—but each one of them got the same goodbye: "Money can't buy love." All three professed theirs to me when they thought they'd lose me, but it didn't change the fact that I didn't love them.

My entire workout, I think about what I want for Luna, and it all comes down to happiness and love.

I can't remember ever feeling as happy as I was with just me and Luna with any woman, but that all changed days ago.

Isabella Steel, what are you doing to me?

* * *

WALKING BACK INTO MY ROOM, I find my bed empty. The food on the tray is untouched, and it irritates me a little because I wanted her to wake up to a meal and smile because I thought of her. It was a first for me.

When I see the balcony door ajar, I head toward it. I hear her voice and push the curtain back.

"It was a great first night."

I stop so I can hear more.

"We're taping today, and I'm sure, after we have a few episodes filmed, the executive producer will shop it." Pause and then she laughs. "No, I'm starting at the bottom. A glorified babysitter for bad boys." She laughs again at whatever the person she's speaking to says. "They're no worse than Dad and our uncles, Kiki." Pause. "Love you, too. Make sure you get those uniforms ironed; school starts—" Pause, and then she gasps, "Katherine, language!"

She's a little momma, I laugh to myself.

"Love you, too. Tell Max to remember he's his own person and not to let the rest of you little thugs push him around." Pause. "Allowing Justice to tattoo my finger wasn't me joining the cult, Kiki. Remember, I'm OG generation next."

Who the fuck is Justice?

She laughs. "It's our secret." Another pause as she looks

over toward the doorway. "I'll email you the itinerary as soon as I get off the phone, shower, and eat breakfast. Bye, Kiki. Love you."

After setting the phone down, she pops her hip out and places her hand on it. "Justice is my cousin."

"I really need to stop thinking out loud." I step out.

She tries not to smile as she rolls her eyes. "You better. Could you imagine?"

I don't hold back my smile. "You motherfuckers get to look at her, but I had my tongue in her pussy last—"

She laughs out loud and smacks me. "I would kill you."

"You may want to, but you wouldn't do that to yourself. I mean, can you imagine laying in my bed tonight, thinking of how much better my fingers are than yours?"

"And who says I'm sleeping in your bed tonight? I'll have fresh linens by then."

"But they won't smell like me."

She quirks an eyebrow. "Right now, you don't smell so hot, Carter."

I narrow my eyes at the sound of my name.

She rolls hers, "Don't look at me like that. I have us planned out."

"Six to nine months of fucking like bunnies in ten different cities? Me, too." She scrunches up her nose, and she blushes. I like it.

"You're putting too much faith in this thing we're doing."

"Is that so?" I ask.

She nods. "It would be the longest secret relationship I've had."

I cock my head to the side, wondering about past relationships and why they've been secrets. "All the others so bad you had to hide them?"

"It was either hide them or hide the bodies." She shrugs. "My father's pretty intense."

"Meaning what?" I feel my fists clench, and she looks down at them.

Her eyes widen, and she shakes her head. "He's protective."

"Then he and I would get along just fine."

"You're not meeting my dad." She laughs as she walks over and steps onto the chair.

"You ashamed of me already?"

She looks back. "No, but he and my mom two are the ones who discovered your little addition to my tattoo. Consider it a favor and do me one—help me out."

I pull her off the chair and carry her ass inside. "You're going to eat, because I've never given a shit if a girl I had in a hotel room got a meal after—"

"I wasn't looking for a meal," she cuts me off. "I was looking for an orgasm."

I drop her on the bed. "You'll get one, maybe two if you're good." I look back at her. "And I know you're good."

"We'll be late." She blushes.

"Oh, hell no, you're still being denied for doing the same to me." I push the food cart over. "I'll feed you breakfast in bed now and my dick for dinner."

I pull the silver dome off one of the plates. "You like eggs, bacon, toast?" I pull the silver dome off the next. "Pancakes and fruit?" And the next. "French toast and pastries?"

She reaches for a piece of bacon.

"A carnivore."

"Mom two is a vegetarian."

She's said that a couple of times now, so I ask, "Mom two?"

She looks at me as she chews, a look that says she's not sure she wants to share.

"Part of your sad story?

She swallows. "We all go through things that we could let ourselves drown in, or we swim. It's just part of my life."

"Care to elaborate?"

"My mom died giving birth to me at eighteen. My maternal grandfather hated my father and fought to keep me. They took him and our family to court until they lost everything. Then, when my dad's father passed away, my father stopped fighting because he felt like it was his fault in a way. I was raised by my mom's parents until my grandfather passed away and my grandmother no longer had to keep me from a man deemed not good enough for me. She knew he was, and she knew her husband was grieving my mother and afraid to let me go."

"It doesn't piss you off?"

She shakes her head. "I'm sorry everyone went through what they did, but that was part of their journey, their sad story. And I'm grateful that my father found someone to even him out." She laughs. "Really grateful."

"Your tattoo, which one is mom two?"

She smiles as she grabs half a hard-boiled egg. "She is love."

When my phone's alarm goes off, I pry my eyes off the vision that is Isabella Steel and see my girl on Facetime. I hit *accept*.

"The sun's up, Daddy. Is the sun up there, too?"

I laugh. "It is, Luna. We're still in the same time zone."

When I stand up and turn, I hear a thud and look back to see Isabella on the floor.

"What was that?" Luna asks.

Bella looks mortified.

I laugh. "It was breakfast."

"You dropped breakfast?"

"Just the best part of it."

"The bacon?"

"Best bacon I've ever tasted."

"Do you think the puppy will like bacon?"

I can't help laughing. "You're persistent." She looks at me like she's a little confused, so I clarify, "Pushy."

"You promised."

"I did, and I won't break my promise."

"Not again?"

My chest tightens. "Not again."

"You going to work?"

"I sure am."

"Love you, Daddy."

"Love you, too, Luna. Give the old lady a hug good morning."

"Talk before bed?"

"How else would I know when the moon was ready to sleep?"

She beams. "Love you, Daddy."

"Love you, Luna, all the way to the moon."

"And back." She smiles.

"Always back."

The call ends, and I walk around to see Bella lying on her back, covering her face.

"Sure, she's right here, Luna. Say hi, Bacon. I mean, Isabella."

She gasps as she uncovers her face, and if looks could kill, I'd be dead.

I toss the phone on the bed and laugh.

The girl must have been a gymnast, because she pops up quicker than shit and pushes me. "That's not funny."

I purposely fall on the bed and bring her down with me.

Before I can say a damn thing, she asks, "Not again. What did she mean when she asked that?"

"Sweet treat, you don't get to know all the things yet." I sit up, bringing her along with me.

"Why?"

I like the way she holds my face, like if she keeps my eyes locked to hers, I'll give her the answer she seeks.

"Because I don't know if I should trust you with everything."

She scowls. "You did some shit to my body without permission, and you don't know if you can trust me?"

"I did, didn't I?"

Her scowl deepens.

I stand up, and she sets her feet on the floor.

"Probably not gonna ask permission for a lot of things I do to your body over the next few months; you'll adjust."

"I'll adjust?" she huffs.

"God, I hope so. I can't wait to slide inside you with no resistance."

"Understood." She shrugs then turns her back to me.

I'm not sure why that makes me uneasy, but it does.

I follow her outside.

Still giving me her back, she says, "Now help me over."

And just like that, she's gone.

* * *

MY CHATS with Luna aren't lengthy, but they're frequent. Morning and evening and sometimes midafternoon. Right now, she's still in school for a couple of weeks, then she starts day camp. Reading is going to be a real struggle, so she's enrolled in a summer enrichment program. Thank

God she loves school, or I'd feel even more like shit than I already do about not being there for her.

After shoving a few more bites to eat in my mouth, I head to the bathroom to shower and get ready for the day.

Walking out of the hotel, I see the line of three SUVs parked and ready for us. I make it just in time to see Bella getting into Mara's vehicle, and the feeling of unease consumes me as I hop in the one leaving behind her.

"Good morning, Tags," David says before putting the vehicle in drive.

I nod. "Let's make it a good one."

FOURTEEN
MAYHEM
BELLA

Sitting in the vehicle with her, I can't help staring at the back of her head and wanting to grab fistfuls of her weave so I can bash her head against the window in hopes of knocking some sense into her. It's bad enough she won't sign the papers and let Tags—Carter—end a marriage she has long abandoned, but the bitch has abandoned her child, too.

"You gotta problem, Izzy?"

You, bitch, my problem is you, and the nearly uncontrollable desire to fuck you up, I think, but just smile instead. "The sun's up, Mara; it's a beautiful day."

I can't see a thing past the lenses of her black sunglasses, but I feel the glare. Oddly, I don't give a damn.

The feeling's mutual, bitch, I think as I look at her.

"So, who's getting the new girl?"

I look over at Grimm. "My name's Bella."

"Fresh meat gets Maze, you, Axel, and Ranger," Mara answers as she guns it through a yellow light.

"You get Neo and Tags?" Grimm, the pasty white, completely bald man with colorfully tattooed skulls, asks.

If you only knew how fucked up that was, Que Ball, I think.

"Not fair, Miss Mayhem."

I look back and see Maze shaking his head.

"It's a non-elimination week," she says dryly. "Plus, it's none of your fucking business, Maze."

"So, it's not just me, huh?" I ask Grimm.

"No, she's a pocket full of posies to all around her."

Pocket full of posies? Um ... weird.

Typically, a producer overseas all aspects of video production, makes executive decisions, and handles getting the money it takes to pull off a show, contracts, and budgeting. I'm too late in the game for that, and in Reality TV, it's different. I'm basically here to pull out the story of the cast members I'm charged with and ... babysit. In order to pull that off, I need them to trust me and be able to open up to me, the client, and make themselves likeable ... or the villain of the show.

"So, it's your studio?" I ask, knowing damn well it is, but I'm making small talk, because this is work, and no matter how much I dislike her, we need to be able to get through several months together. Plus, the old adage, *keep your enemies close*r, isn't used all the time because it's an ineffective way of dealing with them.

"You're a regular Sherlock Holmes, aren't you?" she huffs.

Bitch.

"Does that make you my Watson?"

As the SUV erupts in laughter, she slams on the brakes. "Let's get one thing straight; I'm never gonna be your bitch. You're just filling a position. So, fill it and shut the hell up."

"Easy," Neo says from the passenger seat. "You push

her out and we're delayed even more. I got shit lined up after this thing tanks."

Maze sighs. "The energy in this place is getting negative."

I look back and wink. "You want change, you gotta make it."

Mara hits the gas, and the tires squeal. "I really can't deal with your shit this early in the morning."

I wink at Grimm and whisper, "Do you feel the love? I do. I feel the love."

To that, he smirks and no longer looks so ... grim.

"Tell me about you."

"Why?" he asks, no longer smiling.

"My job is to make sure the real you is shown to the hopefully millions of people watching, in your art and your personality. My job is to help you win."

"I don't care if I win; I just want to work." He turns his head and looks out the tinted window.

Hearing the depth in his voice, it's evident that he has a story, but he offers no more. I don't want to push on day one. I need him to feel comfortable with me, to trust me. So, I give him the emotional space he seems to need.

When the SUV whips into a parking lot then comes to a quick halt, I lean over to look at the brick building that is all black, *like her soul*, I think to myself, with the word *Mayhem* in burgundy script.

I catch what I assume is a smile on her face, but just as quickly as it came, it's gone.

She looks over her shoulder at me and snaps, "What are you looking at?"

I sigh as I look away from her, unbuckle my seatbelt, and open the door. Stepping out in the Florida sun, I can't help noticing the bright and vivid colors—the blue of the sky, the bright, fluffy clouds, the yellow sun, all just beyond the darkness of the building.

"Mind shutting the door so I can lock it?" she snaps.

Kill 'em with kindness, I think as I smile, shut the door to the SUV, and answer, "Sure thing, Mara."

* * *

INSIDE, the cameras are already set up and what I assume are Mara's regular artists—all three female—are at the reception desk, looking just as friendly as her. I introduce myself anyway.

"I'm Bella."

The three of them give me a quick once-over then look away.

When their eyes light up, I look toward the door as David, Breaker, Ranger, Axel, Blade, Darby, Dagger, and Tags come in. I notice the way they look at Tags, like they want to eat him up.

His eyes meet mine, his jaw clenches, and so do my insides. When his Adam's apple bobs, my mouth fills with saliva. He looks away, and I do the same.

Lord, help me, I think as I walk over to Maxine.

She smiles. "Morning."

"Morning." I smile back.

"Any idea who you have?" she asks.

"Maze, Grimm, Axel, and Ranger."

She sucks air in between her teeth. "Four on day one?"

I nod. "I can handle four."

"Yeah?" She looks at me curiously.

"Oh God, not like that!" I laugh.

She shrugs. "I won't judge if you do."

"What would I be judging?" I ask half-joking.

"Twenty-year age difference?" She smirks then whispers, "Daddy issues."

"Well, he's a ..." I look over at him. David is tall, with thick salt and pepper hair, wearing a suit and tie in a tattoo shop. I've seen my own father in the same attire at our family's tattoo shop, Forever Steel, before they handed it over to Kat and Ricco—many times—but David doesn't have the edge that Dad does.

I glance at Tags, who smiles, looks down at the floor, and then glances back at me and catches me staring.

"Fuck, marry, or kill?" Maxine whispers.

"Huh?"

"Which one would you fuck, which one would you marry, and which one would you kill?"

"Are women included?"

She snorts, and all heads swing our way.

David looks at her inquisitively, and she looks at me wide-eyed. We both laugh.

"You ladies, okay?" he asks.

"Stupid question, David," Mara mumbles.

He looks at her blankly then back at Maxine.

She whispers, "Marry," then looks back at him. "We're ready."

"Good," he says, expression unchanged, and then he looks back at the guys.

"And fuck," she whispers. "His wallet isn't the only thing that's huge."

"You little minx." I smirk then nod to the group. "Let's join them."

"She hates me."

"She'll get used to you. Don't change for anyone. Ever."

We join the group.

"Maxine, you have Neo, Dagger, and Darby. Isabella,

you have Maze, Grimm, Axel, and Ranger. Mara, that leaves you with Tags, Blade, and Breaker." He looks up from the list and at Mara. "You're giving her four on day one?"

She shrugs.

"I can handle four."

"Doubtful," Mara mumbles as she walks away. "Pick your first artist. We'll each go one at a time. Fresh meat, since you can handle four, pick two as a warm-up." She looks at Tags. "You first."

"No problem," he says evenly.

I have no idea how he can look at her, let alone be so calm, but he does... he is.

I look back. "Maze and Ranger, you two want to start?"

One of the men with cameras walks up. "I'm Stanley. I'm with you."

"Perfect. Let's capture some amazing moments, shall we?"

* * *

THE THEME for today is mother-daughter tattoos. It's kind of ironic, and I find myself wondering if it hurts Mara at all. She doesn't seem affected.

The first mother-daughter pair are night and day. Maze welcomes them with a kind smile, holding each one's chair as they sit. He's a big guy with a soft heart.

"What brings you two in today?" Ranger asks.

"My daughter's eighteenth birthday." The woman in her thirties blushes as she looks at Ranger, who's clearly ex-military. His arms are heavily tattooed with every type of weaponry you could imagine. Aside from that, he's a walking Ken doll. "I had her at sixteen. No one thought we'd make it. She graduated high school, so I'd say we made it."

"Congratulations." Maze nods. "You should be proud."

I watch Ranger look at Maze with concern. Then back at them. "So, what are you thinking?"

She smiles. "We were hoping for some input."

"The same but different," her daughter adds.

"How about Ranger does one, and Maze the other? The same but different artist interpretations." I smile.

Sitting back I watch as Ranger and Maze draw pictures, shielded from the client and the camera, as they ask personal preferences of mother and daughter. When they finish, both have the other's favorite flower—a rose and a sunflower. The daughter has *Mom* in script beside the stem, and on the opposite side, *You Gave Me Life.* The mother has her daughter's name, and opposite the name is, *You Taught Me Love.* Both women cry when they see what the other chose as script.

It's a beautiful moment, one I'm so glad I am able to witness. Over the years, I have witnessed many of these moments, but this one is different.

After being given their aftercare information, they hug the two men.

I still get a kick out of how people who literally wear a piece of them on their skin are viewed as bad boys. Even these men, ones with criminal records, have huge hearts and enormous talent.

I look over at Tags and see him in deep concentration as he works on the daughter. He looks up briefly and gives me a wink. I'm sure it was so quick no one else but me realized it, a millisecond, but I will definitely scold him for it later.

Or maybe not.

* * *

Tags

THE DAY WENT a fuck of a lot smoother than I expected. When we left the studio, I made damn sure Bella was in the same vehicle as I was. I also made damn sure to snag her phone from her and send myself a text. Why? Because I have plans that involve one Isabella Steel's pussy and my tongue. But first, I need to turn on the charm. She deserves the charm. She more than deserves it.

I shoot her a text.

Me: *Sweets, 1819 70th Street. One hour. Palm trees and a cool breeze. ~ Tag, you're it.*

Bella: *I can't be summoned like a booty call. No... ~ B.S.*

Me: No B.S., I like that idea. Stop playing hard to get. That's another two nights without getting off. ~ Tag, you're ... not getting it.

"Then, why would I come?"

I look over to see her standing on the balcony. She's freshly showered, wrapped in a towel, and looks flushed. The towel wrapped around her hair isn't snug and is falling off.

"Did you just get out of the shower, feeling all powerful because you're naked, throw attitude because of it, then realized you fucked up another chance of getting off and ran out here to make it right?"

She scrunches up her face and averts eye contact. "Pft, n—"

"Don't lie to me, sweet treat, or you're not getting the tongue tonight."

"Don't treat me like a piece of"—she pauses—"ass. And—"

I hold my phone up. "I'm gonna delete this text, pretend it never happened, then try again."

I type out another text.

Me: *Sweets, 1819 70th Street. One hour. Palm trees and a cool breeze. ~ Tag, you're it.*

As I walk back into my room, my phone vibrates.

Bella: *Fine. ~ B.S.*

* * *

STANDING OUTSIDE of Shucker Waterfront Bar and Grill, I look down at my watch. She's a minute late. Any other woman pulled this shit, I'd have left. This one has me sweating and in a fucking suit, leather shoes and shit, clearly trying to impress her and feeling like a fucking idiot.

I reach up to loosen my tie, because it's hot as fuck outside, when a taxi pulls up.

When the door opens and I see her, black dress, short as fuck, with fuck-me heels on, I groan inwardly.

She doesn't even look at me. She looks around, totally missing the fact that I'm right here.

A group of men are checking her out. Can't say as I blame them, but also can't say as my lack of impulse control isn't about to rear its ugly head either.

"Hey, beautiful, no need to look any further," one of the fucks says.

I'm about to pop off at the mouth when she does.

"Do I look like I came here to pick up a man?" She waves her hand over herself.

"Doesn't matter; you found one. A real one. One who wouldn't stand up a pretty little thing like you—"

I walk up to her, and she glances at me out of her peripheral. Then she does a double-take.

I like the way she looks at me.

I hold out my hand. "You ready, sweets?"

She takes it. "Sure am."

I walk to the door and open it. "After you."

"Why thank you."

I let go of her hand and close the door. Then I turn back around and start toward the four assholes.

"When a woman tells you she's got a fucking man—"

I feel soft skin and a tiny hand grabbing mine as she says, "Oh no, you don't."

I turn around and look down at her. "Sweets, please go inside—"

"If I can deal with *her*, you can handle walking away from them. No harm, no foul."

"Disrespecting you—"

"You're disrespecting my belly. Come on, I'm hungry."

When we walk inside, the hostess looks at me. "Can I help you?"

"You can help us. Reservations under Taggant."

I look at Bella. "Outside, under the palm trees, in the breeze, okay?"

She smiles and nods. "Yeah, perfect."

With my hand on the bare skin of her lower back, we follow the hostess through the dimly lit restaurant and onto the deck.

Outside, the breeze blows perfectly, so the humidity isn't that bad, even in this fucking suit. Well worth it, though, to see her eyes light up.

I pull out her chair, and she smiles over her shoulder at me as she sits.

God damn, I sigh to myself.

I take off my jacket and throw it over the back of the chair, push it closer to her, and sit.

She bites her lip and looks down as the waitress pours us water.

"Can I get you two anything to drink?"

"I'm good with water. My lady would like a glass of—"

"I'm good with water, too."

The waitress smiles. "I'll give you a few minutes to look over the menu."

As soon as she walks away, Isabella looks around. "We're a bit overdressed."

"You're overdressed in just a sheet."

She smiles. "You look good in a suit."

"I look good in you."

She nods. "This is true."

The waitress reappears and asks, "You all decide what you want?"

"I know exactly what I want. How about you, Isabella? Do you know what you want?"

She looks up at the waitress. "New York Strip, medium please."

I can't help laughing. "I'll have the same."

We watch the boats dock as we eat and, fuck, she can eat.

"You eat that steak like I'm gonna eat your pussy tonight."

She laughs. "You think you bring me to dinner and you're automatically going to get laid?"

"No, sweets, but I'm going to make dessert out of you."

FIFTEEN

VEGAS

TAGS

Lying in bed next to a sleeping Isabella, I look out at the city lights.

Vegas.

I need to address some shit here. I need the papers signed.

When she skates her hand across my chest and sighs contently in her sleep, I'm thinking tequila, Elvis, and white wedding chapels, oddly placed throughout the city. Probably a good thing I'm legally hitched, or that tattoo would be the least of her worries.

Is it possible to look at someone and know you want them in your life permanently? Yes.

Can it last? I'm thinking I'm going to fuck my way through the next few months with her in my bed every night to make sure of it, and not for me—I already know—but for her.

She is ... mine.

When my phone goes off, reality kicks me square in the balls and Isabella jumps up.

"The moon?"

"The sun." I laugh as I kiss the top of her head and roll out of bed.

She's up, sheet wrapped around her hot little bod, and then down on the floor.

"Get your fine ass back in bed. I'll take the bathroom."

"This is stupid."

Over my shoulder, I tell her, "Don't say that shit again."

I hit the light in the bathroom then *accept*.

"The sun's up, Daddy. Is the sun up there, too?"

"Not yet, Luna. We're in a different time zone now."

"For how long?" She seems a bit worried.

"Two weeks is all. But after Vegas, I have a whole week, remember?"

"You gonna work at Sisco's?"

"Not if I'm still on the tour."

"If you go to work at Sisco's, can I go with you?"

"Not a great place for little Lunas."

"But, Daddy," she whines.

It's not normal for her to whine.

"You tired, baby girl?"

She nods.

"Did you eat breakfast yet?"

She shakes her head.

"Well, you better fuel-up, get fired-up, and get crazy excited about learning something new."

"We don't learn anything; we clean the stupid classroom. And it's hot and—"

"You love school, Luna. Some days aren't going to be as fun as others. We take the good with the bad, and we bust behind to get to more good."

She nods.

"So get through it to get to the good."

"Like a box of cereal with a prize at the bottom?"

I smile. "Exactly like that."

"You going to get a break?"

"If things go good, I may be able to get back for a few suns and moons. But it's not a promise, okay?"

"Love you, Daddy."

"Love you, too, Luna. Give the old lady a hug good morning."

"Talk before bed?"

"How else would I know when the moon was ready to sleep?"

"Love you, Daddy."

"Love you, Luna, all the way to the moon."

"And back." She smiles.

"Always back."

When I walk out of the bathroom and into the room, she's in bed with her back toward me, little spoon style.

"How old is she?"

"Almost four." I slide in next to her and pull her tightly to me.

"Why is she already in school?" she asks on a yawn.

This wasn't a conversation I wanted to have yet, but fuck it. "She had some developmental delays. Wanted to nip it in the bud. Head start program, and she's pretty much on track."

She rolls over and looks at me. "What kind of delays?"

"She lucked out. Just some balance and coordination issues. Difficulty with attention; a bit hyper."

"She lucked out how?"

"It's late, not a great time to start this conversation." *And already knowing you, not even sure it needs to happen, sweet treat*, I think.

"Okay," she says, rolling to her side, her back to me.

"Is okay like fine in woman talk?"

"Nope," she says.

Enough said. It is exactly like fine, confirmed with a sharp *nope*.

I wrap my arm around her and cup her breast. Her nipple immediately tightens under my fingers. "There's something else I'd like to talk about."

She whimpers and arches her back, pressing into my hand. "And what's that?"

"Your tasty tits." I move over her, as she rolls onto her back. In one move, the covers are gone and I'm sucking sweet tit.

"Okay," she moans as she fists my hair.

Pulling her nipple out with my teeth, I reach between her legs and spread her soaked pussy with my fingers. "Fucking edible."

"I want you inside me." She rocks against my touch.

I release her tit and look at her. "I said one more nig—"

She pulls my cock from my shorts, stopping me from continuing, and rubs her thumb across my head. "Stop playing hard"—she squeezes my dick—"to get and fuck me."

Before I verbally agree, she rubs my cock against her wet, hot opening. "I'm on the pill. Are you clean?"

My heart hammers in my chest, my balls catch fire, and I shove into her with the force of a man whose balls have been blue for two torturous nights. "I'm fucking clean."

Her mouth is open, and she's trying to suck in air.

"Fuck." I pull out. "Sorry, sweet treat. I should have licked—"

She narrows her eyes. "Do it again."

So, I do.

After a few hard, fast, and breathtaking strokes in her tight as fuck pussy, she begins to meet me thrust for thrust.

"Fuck yes," I groan before bowing my head and taking

one of her tits in my mouth, sucking so hard that she cries out.

Her clenched pussy is getting wetter. She's on the verge of coming.

Releasing her tit, I demand, "Fucking give it to me." I slam into her. "Come all over my cock, sweets." I slam in again.

Her head is almost against the headboard.

Slam.

"Feel so fucking good being inside you raw."

Slam.

"Never gonna want it any other way."

Slam.

Never gonna want any other pussy after this, I think.

Slam.

"Harder!" she cries.

Slam.

She digs her nails into my back. "Faster," she begs.

Slam.

She slams her hands onto the mattress and grips the sheets, her back arching, and she cries out my name, my real name, "Carter! Oh God, yes!"

"Oh no, sweets." I grip her hips and fuck her until she remembers. "What's my name?"

"Oh God." Her voice is gravely, throaty, sexy. Her thighs tremble.

"What's my fucking name?" I slam into her harder, faster as my balls tighten, burn.

"Carter!" she cries. Her body tenses, she trembles, and then she cries out again. "Carter! Mine!"

"Well, fuck." I sigh, balls deep inside her.

When she looks at me, there is obvious confusion, mixed with embarrassment.

"Don't do that." I give up the thought of filling her up and bend to kiss her.

"Sorry," she mumbles against my lips, panting, still trembling.

"Don't be sorry." I say against hers. "Never sounded better."

She grabs my hair and yanks my head back. "I like your name."

"I like being yours."

"I didn't mean—"

"Shut it, Isabella Steel. You and I know exactly what you meant."

Her eyes search between mine, and fuck if she doesn't look scared.

"I won't hurt you, sweets."

"I'm not worried about me; I'm worried about you."

I laugh, but she looks dead fucking serious.

"I'm a big boy." I slam into her as a reminder. "I know what I'm getting into." I pull out slowly then slam in again.

"You have no—"

Slam.

"You worry about how sore you'll be for the rest of the day while I think about filling your cunt with my cum."

Slam.

Slam.

Slam.

"Oh, fuck yes!" she cries.

"Again, sweets?" I hiss.

"Shut up and fuck me." She sinks her nails into my ass, and I commence to doing just that.

"My fucking pussy."

Slam, slam, slam.

"Yours!" she cries. "Oh my God, it's so yours!"

And I lose my shit, all up inside her.

Face down, buried in her hair, I feel undone in a way I've never fucking felt.

Have I lost it before? Yeah.

Like this? No fucking way.

"Tags?" she whispers.

"Yeah, sweets?" I whisper back.

"You're hard again."

I push up on my elbows and cup her face. "Your lucky morning."

"Are you kidding me right now?"

Slam.

* * *

I WAKE up to her head on my chest, her leg wrapped around me, the smell of sex, sweet fucking sex, around us, and my cock in her hand.

"Fuck yes," I mumble and wrap my hand around hers.

"What? Huh? Is it the phone?" she whines.

I tighten my grip on our hands. "Yeah, and it's for you."

She blinks rapidly and opens her eyes.

I stroke my cock with her hand. "The bone phone."

A laugh erupts from her. "What are you? Twelve?"

"It's an important call, sweets." I roll her to her back and hover over her. "You should definitely ... take it."

"I couldn't take it again if you dumped a bucket of KY between my legs."

Kissing her neck, I laugh.

With her hands on my shoulders, she sinks her nails into them as I kiss down between her breasts.

"Don't you dare." She pouts.

"Just a taste."

"I have to go—oh ..."

"Mmm ..."

"Okay, okay, okay, that's ... that's ..." She fists my hair. "Right there."

I can't help laughing as she grinds against my face.

After a few licks, I ask, "How'd we get here from bone phone?"

"FaceTime," she moans.

SIXTEEN
OR BUST...
BELLA

Sitting across the hotel's restaurant, a few minutes early for the production meeting, I watch the guys across the room. Specifically, I watch Carter and the relaxed way in which he sits, the easy smile, the way he interacts with the rest of them. All easy.

And to think I thought maybe I had daddy issues. He's nothing like Dad, and I like it. I like it a lot.

He glances over at me and gives me one of those millisecond long winks that I know is just for me.

How the hell do I know it's just for me? I scold myself. I've known him for all of ten freaking days.

Ten fucked-up days.

Ten.

Perfect ten.

Ten pierced inches of pleasure.

That tongue.

God.

That face.

Those lips.

The eyes.

The body.

The ink.

The fucking nose ring.

Him.

Ten.

The perfect ten.

A chair beside me slides out, and I look up. "Hey, Maxine."

"Did you get enough rest?" She kisses my cheek.

Rest? I laugh to myself.

"Plenty," I lie.

"That's a good thing. We have a lot to get through the next two weeks. Mara said there wasn't shit in the tapes from Miami."

"What?" I gasp.

"Said it was all a waste," David answers.

"Even Maze and Ranger's work? I loved the interaction between them and the mother-daughter pair they worked on. It was—"

He interrupts, "She said—"

"Can I have a look?"

I feel Maxine kick me under the table.

"This is her deal. Her baby," He states.

I bite back words that beg to be uttered: *Her baby is almost four*.

He continues, "She has a lot riding on this. She wants what's best for the show."

"But to totally ditch two weeks of work?"

"None of your concern."

I look up as Mara sits down.

I have to bite my tongue to keep from telling her what I actually think about her. And only because her clueless father is sitting here. Otherwise, I could give a shit less about the woman who ditched her kid and is holding Carter hostage.

"Vegas is a good place to kick this off. Bright lights, big city."

If I didn't hate her, I'd tell her that's a great idea for the episode's name, but change *big* to *sin*. Alas, I despise her, so she can suck my spirit dick.

"House of Ink is hosting still, correct?" David asks.

She nods. "We start tomorrow. Appointments are being taken for the couples."

"Couples getting married?" I ask.

She looks over at me then away.

"At least twenty?" David asks.

"In the next two days."

"You sure they can handle it?"

"They're going to have to. They're going to get two days after that before we hit Tattoo and Blues, then two days before we move to Ink Incorporated."

"You sure they can handle it?" David asks again.

"They can or they can go," she says flippantly.

"Three studios in twelve days." I nod. "I think they can handle it. I remember—"

"Nobody cares about your roots, Barbie." Mara sighs.

"Mara," David warns, "we're a team."

"No, she's a handler."

I look at David. "It's just fine with me. I get a producer credit on my resume."

He nods.

"Teams, I think we should change them up," David suggests.

"No," Mara says. "I like where we left it in Miami."

He looks around the table. "We all good with that?"

"I am, as long as we get a look at the footage and can cut our own scenes."

"That's not your call," Mara snaps.

"I'm going to agree with her." David finally blocks her unfair reign.

"Fine," Mara snaps then waves over a waitress. "A bottle of—"

"How about some orange juice," David says sternly.

She glares at him. "I had pill issues, not alcohol."

"It's one in the afternoon, Mara."

I cut in, "What time do we meet in the morning?"

"Ten a.m.," David answers. "The cars will be outside."

"Perfect."

"You look tired," Maxine whispers.

I have no idea how David heard her, but he did. "I'm sure we're all tired. Time change is never easy, even a couple hours. Feel free to order room service. I think we've covered everything here."

"Excellent. Thanks so much." I stand up, give Maxine a shoulder squeeze, and tell David, "Have a great night."

I walk over to the table where the guys are sitting. "Maze, Ranger, Grimm, Axel, what do you guys say we have some fun?"

I feel piercing, hazel eyes on me.

"How about the rest of us?" Blade asks.

"You're not mine. They are." I look at Maze, who's looking at Tags. "You wanna go see Vegas?"

"Yeah." He grins. "Yeah, I do."

"You haven't eaten yet," Tags says sternly then looks at me. "Have you?"

He knows I haven't.

I shrug, "Not all that hungry."

"You ever see Axel when he hasn't eaten?"

I look at Axel; long, curly hair pulled up in a bun, dark green eyes.

"I tend to get a little hangry."

Tags continues, "Grimm here needs to beef up. Ranger is an eating machine. You'll spend more time searching for all-you-can-eat buffets than doing whatever it is you have planned. And Maze would follow a pretty woman around until his feet fell off, unless he could get into a car. And mind you, the fool doesn't have his license."

I look at Maze, who shrugs. "Beautiful women are my weakness."

"The bigger, the better, huh, man?" Neo jokes.

"I'd rather have something to hold onto than a bag of bones." He looks at Grimm. "No offense, man."

"Wasn't gonna fuck her, just needed to see her," he sneers.

I'm not sure I even want to know what the hell that's all about, but it gives me the creeps.

"We know, man." Tags nods. "We know."

Tags looks at me. "You could join us. Some of us might be on your team in the future. We may be worth getting to know, too."

"How hard are you right now?" Neo asks him.

Tags looks over at him. "You wanna come over here and give it a squeeze?"

"Pretty boys, always coming out of the closet around me." Neo laughs.

Like the winks I get, I swear I see him smirk at Neo, and then it's gone.

"You gay, man?" Axel asks.

"If by gay, you mean happy, then yeah, I'm gay as fuck." Tags winks at him, and not the kind of wink he gives me.

He looks up at me. "So, what do you say, Isabella? Sit with us?"

"If my guys are staying, so am I."

I glance over and see Mara glaring at me. Then I look back and smile inwardly when I see the seat next to Neo is open.

When I sit by him, he laughs. "Was it something I said?"

"Are you talking about the pig statement you made to me in Miami or the fact you basically admitted you have a crush on Tags?"

The table erupts in laughter.

He narrows his eyes. "What the fuck are you talking about?"

"Don't worry, Neo; I see you."

"Again, what the fuck are you talking about?" He shakes his head.

"No judgment, Neo, none. We can be friends now that I know you're not interested in my kind."

"I've been fucking Mara since Miami," he says loud enough to ensure the table heard it.

"Like I said ..." I shrug.

Everyone laughs, and Tags looks down. I don't know why that bothers me, but it does.

Annoyed, I add, "You may want to step up the pace, wear her out, or at least get her off. She may be less bitchy."

Neo smirks. "You giving me advice on how to fuck?"

"I'm just asking you to do us all a favor. No one in this entire restaurant's attitude screams *I need to come* like that one."

My phone vibrates in my pocket, and I pull it out.

Tags: *Kill the conversation or she won't be the only one not coming. ~ Tags*

"Who's that?" Neo tries to look at my phone.

"Apparently, my father," I say, shoving it back in my pocket.

It vibrates again.

I ignore it.

Again.

"You're pissing Daddy off, little girl. Better respond."

Tags: *I'm not fucking around, Bella. You wanna talk fucking to another guy? Expect it back. ~ Tags*

Tags: *I see how it is. ~ Tags*

Me: *Okay, Dad. ~ B.S.*

SEVENTEEN
THE STRIP
TAGS

I don't get pissed off too often, but I've been pissed off since Bella took off with her team.

When the rest of the group starts to disperse and Neo and I are left alone for the first time since the fight in Miami, I sit back, cross my arms, and look at him.

"David might be fucking clueless, man, but I'm not. You wanna tell me the real reason you're here?"

"I'll tell you the same thing I did in Miami—it's none of your business."

"No?" He laughs.

"No. It's between her and me."

"You like that position, don't you?"

"The fuck is that supposed to mean?" I laugh. "If I remember correctly, you're the one who wanted to take a knee for me."

That pisses him off, which was the point.

"You can't stand that she chose me over you and the kid she didn't want."

I grip the arms of the chair to hold myself back from busting his fucking face. "First, you keep my daughter out of your thoughts and words. Second, you see me trying to get with her, telling her daddy her secret, going after her in any fucking way?"

"I see you here, and I see what it's doing to her."

"What the fuck do you care what it does to her? You're hitting on the new girl." *My girl.*

"Not that it's any of your fucking business, but Mara and I haven't changed; we still like a third once in a while."

"I don't give a damn. I have business with her. When it's concluded, you can fuck the hell out of each other, pop fucking pills till you can't remember your names, and fuck with a third, fourth, or fifth. I don't give a damn." I stand up and place my hands on the table. "You and me, we've been done for years. I got no beef with you, so don't bring it to me."

"You better remind yourself you chose that kid—"

I reach across the table and grab his throat. "You shut the fuck up."

I see two men in suits walking our way and let go of him.

"There a problem over here?" It's security.

"None whatsoever," I say then walk the fuck away.

WALKING OUT OF THE RESORT, I look around and see Blade and Breaker smoking. I walk over. "One of you have a spare?"

Blade nods as he reaches into his pocket then taps one out of the pack.

"Thanks, man," I say as he gives me a light. Blowing out the smoke, I ask, "You see where they went?"

Breaker shakes his head. "Nah, but I wouldn't worry too

much about it. We're good. Mayhem clearly stacked the teams."

He's not wrong, but she is for doing so.

"Just new girl and her guys?" I ask, playing it cool.

"No, Dagger and Darby, too."

I take another drag and shake my head. Blowing out the smoke, I ask, "They say where they're going?"

Breaker laughs. "Some shit about fountains, flowers, and street performers. Pretty sure they were just looking around the strip."

"Darby asked about strip clubs. She didn't seem opposed." Blade winks. "I bet she's a freak in the sheets."

"Girl like that probably just lays there." I toss my smoke in the ashtray. "Heard she was a lesbian."

"No shit?" Blade asks.

"She sure as fuck doesn't look like it."

"Just what I heard." I shrug.

"Probably why she was good with the strip club idea, man." Blade puts his smoke out.

"Love to see her get a lap dance." Breaker starts walking. "Let's go check it out."

IN FRONT OF THE BELLAGIO, in a crowd of hundreds, I spot her.

The guys are all standing in front of a fountain, half of them shirtless.

"She may like to lick pussy, but it appears she may like to at least look at a half-naked man."

As we get closer, I see that she's taking pictures.

I hang back and watch as she directs them, moving

between group shots and individual. Then I see her talking to Blade. He turns around and waves for me to come over.

"Fuck." I sigh when I see her looking at me. "Busted."

I walk over, and she tells me to get in the group shot. And I decide, *fuck it*.

I peel my shirt off. Not for nothing, I spend a fuck of a lot more time in the gym than most of these guys and it shows.

"Tags, Ranger, and Blade, down in front," she says as she holds her phone camera out and snaps pictures. "Could you loosen up, act like you're having fun?"

I hold my fingers up in an *L* shape and smile. A ghost of a smile crosses her pretty lips, and then it's gone.

"Okay, you three, Blade, Breaker, and Tags, I need individual shots."

A crowd seems to be gathering around and watching us. I look at Maze and nod at them. He turns and looks around.

"Okay, men, let's go check out the flowers."

"What about the strip club?" Blade asks.

She shrugs. "Feel free, but you'll miss out on the exposure."

Three hours later, and we've followed her little ass around Vegas while she's snapped a million photos in front of the most recognizable locations in the city.

"Who's up for drinks?" she asks.

* * *

TWO HOURS LATER, we're at a rooftop bar called Inspire. There's a DJ playing and, apparently, it's ladies drink free night. She's done about seven shots and is leaning against the bar, smiling and shaking her ass to the music, but with reserve. That reserve ends when a song comes on that she clearly likes.

Holding up her glass of something pink, she sashays her ass onto the dance floor, right in the middle of a bunch of chicks who look like they're on Daddy's dime.

Easy, baby, I think, watching her try to blend in with the type of girls who don't let others in.

After a couple minutes, I'm eating my words. She's blending in with the Beverlys.

"Sweet, but psycho," Blade yells over the music. "Told you she was a closet freak."

When she takes her button-up off and ties it around her waist, I groan at the sight of her in a tight-ass, white tank. Then, when she pulls her hair out of the top-knot, messy bun and shakes her hair out while shaking her ass, I start to get hard.

I watch her dance for three songs all while sipping on iced water and willing my cock to stay the fuck down.

When the music changes to a slow beat, I see some fucking douche walk up and ask her to dance.

"Oh damn," Axel says behind his fist in front of his mouth. "She's gonna be late in the morning."

"Well, we can't let that shit happen, can we?" I ask as I walk onto the dance floor, tap on the guy's shoulder, and glare as I shake my head.

Fucker looks like he's about to piss his khakis.

"You sent him away, you better dance with me, Carter!" She throws her hands in the air and closes her eyes. Then she starts singing at the top of her lungs.

"I don't dance," I yell over the music.

" *'But I feel safe here. Lay with me. The stars watch us tonight. That's okay with me. Tell me all your secrets till the sun comes up—'* "

"Fuck ..." I groan as I step toward her.

" '*Place my hand by your heart tonight. Feel your heart beat as we shut our eyes.*' " She opens her eyes and smiles a big, sloppy yet sexy as fuck smile. " '*Show me all your pictures of how we fell in ...*' " She stops and her eyes widen. "Oops."

"Sweets, this isn't keeping shit quiet."

"I was gonna dance with that dude, but you—"

"Like fuck you were."

"If I wanna, I will." She shakes her head. "But I don't wanna."

"Good fucking thing."

"You should definitely not kiss me right now."

"No shit, sweets. Probably shouldn't be sporting wood either, but you had to go and make it happen."

"My fault, huh?"

"Well, it sure as fuck wasn't Maze's."

"What about all the girls around here?"

"You think I see anyone but you, you're wrong. Let me know when all you see is me."

She pouts out her bottom lip. "That was so sweet."

"No, what it is, is fucked up. You're doing shit to me, Isabella Steel. Shit that hasn't been done."

"FaceTime?" She grins.

"I'm trying to be pissed at you right now."

She smiles. "It's difficult, huh?"

"I don't like games."

"And I don't like telling the guy who did shit to my back, who shouldn't have been forgiven yet was, that his sexy as fuck face and his big, pierced dick is all I'm interested in riding."

"You have a filthy mouth," I say, looking at it.

"You wanna make it filthier?"

"Fuck," I growl as I nod.

"We can do that, too." She licks her lips.

"Let's get the fuck out of here."

EIGHTEEN
GO TIME
BELLA

I wake to a call and a banging head.

"Hello?"

"Time to get that ass outta bed, sweets."

"Huh?"

"Unless you're glued to it after last night's activities."

"What are you talking about?" I moan and roll onto my back.

"Beggin' to have your ass pounded, didn't realize I was—"

"WHAT!" I shoot up.

He laughs. "You awake now?"

"You better not have touched—"

"If my cock was in your ass, you'd feel it still, sweets. You passed out on my chest after promising every filthy deed in the book. Some not even in the book. Not yet anyway."

"What?" I ask again.

"The sun's up, sweets, and it's a beautiful day to make art."

" 'Kay."

“ ’Kay?”

“Uh-huh.” I yawn and start to laugh as I lie back down.

“Do I need to come wake you up, or are you good?”

“Am I good?”

“The best.”

“Wasn’t really asking—”

“Bottle of water and some Tylenol on your nightstand. Then shower. You have forty minutes.”

“Oh shit,” I gasp.

* * *

WHEN I GET to the studio, I see my guy Stanley with his camera all set and ready.

“You drink your coffee black?” I ask, handing him a cup.

“I do today.” He takes it and says, “Thanks.”

“What’s your regular?” I ask before taking a sip of mine.

“Two creams, one sugar.”

“Nothing fancy then?”

He shakes his head. “Nah.”

“Our party girl made it.” Ranger laughs.

“Girl’s a singer, too,” Axel taunts.

Maze looks back at me. “And a dancer.”

“Don’t you guys have anything else to do but harass the help?” I shake my head at them.

“We get to fuck up some lives for the next two weeks.” Axel laughs. “Two people who have the drunken delusions of happy ever afters in a city known for quickie weddings.”

“You got married in Vegas, yeah?” Ranger asks.

“Fuck you.” Axel gives him a finger.

“Get it out of your system now, boys. It’s almost show time.”

Leaving them behind, I walk over to where David

stands with some of the crew. "Could I talk to you for a minute?"

He looks at me and nods.

"I helped with a fundraising event up in Syracuse, New York, an online bachelor auction of sorts. I had the idea of maybe pumping up some social media around the show. Kind of a meet-the-cast thing."

He doesn't say anything, so I pull out my phone, hit the app, open the folder I had stored the pictures in, and hand it to him. "I took some pictures around the city last night and could start some social media accounts or help clean theirs up. Only a couple have them and—"

"That's already on the list of shit to do," a voice from behind interrupts me. "When this show gets picked up, they'll want to do that themselves."

David looks at his daughter and nods. "Good." Then he walks away from me.

I turn around and look up at her. "Wouldn't hurt to start building up the—"

"Bella," Tags interrupts me. "Got a minute?"

What the hell?

"Isn't he yours?" I ask her.

"You have no idea." She rolls her eyes and walks away.

I turn to see Tags standing there.

"You look better than I thought you would after last night."

I look around to see if anyone else heard him. They didn't.

"Did you hear what that bitch just said to me?" I snarl.

"Easy, sweets. Do me a favor?"

I nod.

"Keep all those ideas to yourself. She's not buying one of them."

"Then why am I even here?"

"I think you know why." He gives me a millisecond wink then walks away.

* * *

AFTER THE FIRST WEEK, I realize he was right. Nothing I offer creatively is taken seriously. The footage I spend hours going over and picking what's best for my artists are always discarded by the bitch. And David, well, he doesn't even look at the work I pour myself into creating, "It's her baby," is always his response.

But it doesn't stop me.

The days we aren't in studios, Stanley and I are in front of our laptops, cutting footage of heartfelt stories of people in love. The guys joke about covering up a piece you no longer want being harder than actually getting divorced.

I learned a lot about each of them, and they no longer look at me like I'm some flighty little debutante, taking a job for a paycheck to impress Daddy. They know I'm working for them, and they are working for me.

I'm about to close my laptop, knowing Carter ... Tags—I shake my head and smile when realization hits that he's only Carter when we're alone—when I get a notification that I have a FaceTime request from Dad. I accept it.

"You look beautiful, Little Bell, but are you sleeping at all?"

I lean in and look at myself. I have circles under my eyes.

"I'm good, Dad, just frustrated."

"About what?"

I unleash all the anger inside of me for that bitch and her dad for not caring about the show. "And the show is about the guys, Dad, not about just the amazing work these men have done. But ..." I stop because, if I tell him they're all ex-cons, he may lose his shit.

"But your heart got involved in a game of elimination."

He's not wrong, but in games where hearts are involved, secrets are kept, and lies are told, it's hard to be objective.

"What is it, Little Bell?"

I fight back the words I want to say.

"The truth."

I miss our caring dysfunction, is what I want to say, but I go with, "I miss you guys."

He nods once. "Not often I went a week without meeting you for dinner. Been nearly three, Little Bell. Didn't like the way you left either. Too quick."

"We have a break coming up. I'll be home."

"When?"

"As soon as this wraps."

"Two days?" he asks.

"Holy fucking shit," I gasp, and his eyes nearly hit his desk. "Sorry, Daddy, but two days!"

He frowns. "Yeah."

I feel my face falling, too, but I pull it up into a smile. "I'll see you soon then."

"Little Bell, you know the saying *what happens in Vegas stays in Vegas*?"

I nod.

"Do me a favor and leave the language in Vegas."

I cover my face so he doesn't see me laugh.

"I love you, Isabella. See you soon."

He disconnects. He never disconnects. Something's wrong. I feel myself begin to panic. Something is off in Jersey.

Something is … I laugh. I swore. He's mad. He'll get over it. We're two days from wrapping up Vegas.

Sitting at my desk, I try to finish editing the video Stanley and I were putting together. I decided full steam ahead on my idea. It may not be used for the show, but I bet it would mean a lot to everyone in the cast.

After a few hours, I realize I forgot to eat, something Tags seemed to remind me that I needed to do these past couple weeks.

"Gotta fuel up to fuck, sweets."

Two more nights in his arms, two more mornings waking up to his sexy self and his sensitive side. Then a week where he gets to say goodnight to the moon with his sweet little girl, and I get to spend time with my family.

I send Stanley the email of what I've done. It'll have to do for now.

Two more sleeps, Bella. I sigh as I stand up while closing my computer. Then I shower in hopes of meeting Tags a little earlier than our usual midnight.

When I step out of the room and head toward the elevator, I get snagged from behind and dragged down the hall. I'm about ready to yell at Tags when I see him coming out of his room.

"Hey!"

When he starts laughing, I hear Ranger's voice. "Just let it happen, Little Bell."

Little Bell. He called me Little Bell.

"What are you doing?"

"We're gonna party like tomorrow's not a guarantee." He laughs.

" 'Cause it isn't." Maze chuckles.

When they open a door and pull me in, I see Axel.

He pops a bottle of champagne. "Let's drink!"

Ranger and Maze, each of who have had one arm looped around mine as they dragged me down the hall, split ways, each one taking a side of the bed as the drag me onto it.

Sitting cross-legged, I see Grimm walk out of the bathroom. I'm shocked by his appearance. His face is no longer dusted with some sort of powder, his eyes no longer outlined in black, and his hair isn't slicked back and stuck to his head.

"Well, damn, Grimm, look at you."

He gives me a one-shoulder shrug. "Got a date with a girl."

"Hired a hooker," Maze whispers. Thankfully, Grimm doesn't hear him.

I hold back my laugh. "Good for you."

I slide off the bed and walk over to grab the glass Axel is holding out for me. I see Stanley at the door, holding the camera, taping us.

"This is awesome." I hold up my glass. "Cheers."

"Wait. We gotta make a toast."

They all grab a flute and hold it up. And I wait ... and wait.

"Someone going to say something?" Axel whispers.

They all look at each other, and I can't help laughing. "I've heard a million of these things at Sunday dinner with the family but never led one, so take it easy on me afterward, got it?"

"Sure thing, Little Bell." Maze winks.

"May our friendship be as permanent as the art you all drew. May we look back on these precious memories that bound this little crew. To art and ink and the friends whose glasses we clink."

We all tap our glasses together then I take a sip while the rest of them slam theirs down.

"So, it's gonna be like that, huh?" I laugh and raise my glass. "Well, bottoms up."

I watch Ranger pour a shot of Patron and look at the time. It's only one in the afternoon. Plenty of time to recover.

I grab a shot, hold it up, and say, "Forever Steel."

They all do the same, then Ranger asks, "What the hell is Forever Steel?"

"It's not a what; it's a way of life." I shrug. "It's loyalty, it's truth, it's the love of a family by blood and by choice. It's Forever Steel."

"So, another shot then?" Maze asks.

"Hell yes!" I laugh as I look over them. "Hell yes."

After a few shots, I'm dizzy as hell.

"Any chance there's chips or something in here?"

"Some healthy shit of Ranger's in the fridge under the bar," Axel says, pouring another shot. "Help yourself."

Bending down, I look in the tiny fridge. Apples, oranges, hard boiled eggs. Nothing sounds good. Then I spot candy. I pull the baggy out, open it, reach inside, and then pop a few in my mouth.

"You can't hide sugar from an emotional eater."

Axel, Ranger, Maze, and Grimm all look at me.

"I found your candy."

Ranger swallows hard. "You eat any yet?"

"I'm gonna eat the whole damn bag." I laugh, reaching inside.

Maze jumps forward and snatches the bag.

"Damn, Maze, I haven't seen you move that fast this whole time."

"You eat a lot of them?" Axel asks, his face now as white as Grimm's normally is.

"A few. Why?"

Ranger scowls. "How many's a few?"

I swallow the last of the chewed-up gummies. "How the hell would I know? And why are you all acting so weird?"

Axel sighs. "Dump and count, man."

Maze dumps the bag on the table and begins counting. Then he starts counting again.

Freaking out, I grab the bag that he tossed on the floor and look at it.

Blazed Goods.

"Blazed ...?" I pause when I remember seeing the name on the side of a food truck. Then I remember when I thought it was donuts, and Tags told me, "It might be, but I'm guessing it's the special ingredient that gives it the name." When it didn't click, he laughed at me. "Edibles, sweets."

I look up, and they're all looking at me.

"How fucked up am I going to be?"

"Pretty fucked up. You ate three." Grimm actually laughs.

I try to stay calm, but then I remember one hit off a pipe in undergrad to mark off one of Dad's Ds, I was fucked up pretty good. "Am I going to get sick? Die? What the fuck is going to happen to me?"

Maze smirks. "Pretty good chance it'll start with paranoia."

"Maze, you're the one I trust most; please do not make a joke about this right now."

"No joke, Little Bell; you're gonna be *so* fucked up."

I look at the bag. " '*Recommended usage: no more than*

two in a four-hour period. No more than four a day. Keep refrigerated and—' "

"Gimme that." Grimm snatches the bag then swipes the gummies on the table and into the bag.

"Seriously, guys, have any of you taken three of these at a time, like ever?" I look around and shake my head.

Grimm reaches into the bag and pulls some out. He opens his hand, revealing three, then pops them into his mouth and swallows them without even chewing. "I have."

This is bad. This is so fucking bad.

"Dude, what the fuck?" Axel snatches the bag.

"I'm not gonna be a bitch and let her do it alone."

I slap my palm against my forehead. "Grimm, I wish you had."

"Your date tonight?" Maze whispers, but we all hear him.

"Fuck." Grimm runs his hand through his hair. "Well, I got a few hours. Let's see how it goes."

I hear the door open as I watch Axel move to the fridge, toss them in, and kick the door shut. When I look back, Blade and Breaker are walking in, and behind them, Tags is carrying an armful of pizza.

This is going to be so *fucking bad.*

"We're here to celebrate."

Ranger sighs. "Shit."

NINETEEN
BLAZING
TAGS

"This is a joke, right?" I ask for the second time since the idiots told me that Isabella was about to take flight.

"Nope." Grimm grins. It's fucking creepy seeing him acting more human than corpse. Add that smile, and it's not just creepy; it's downright disturbing.

I hurry to the bathroom and pound on the door.

"We're in here right now. Please hold."

Taking a chance that it's not locked; I turn the knob and open the door.

"Who's we?"

"Me and her." She throws her thumb over her shoulder at the mirror.

"That's your reflection, Bella."

"Call me, Little Bell." She grins, and not creepily like Grimm, but not the normal, I'm-a-badass-little-seductress-and-I'm-gonna-fuck-a-hole-in-your-heart-with-my-spirit-dick Isabella either. She pouts out her bottom lip. "Okay, but they call me it, and everyone else does, too. Well, not here, but home. My daddy calls me Little Bella, and Cyrus, and Zandor, and Xavier, and Momma Joe, and Momma Carly, and Aunt Tara, and Aunt—"

"Okay, Dorothy, just a heads-up, you're gonna feel like you're not in Kansas anymore, but you're gonna be fine in a few hours. Best thing for you to do is chill the fuck out and—"

She pushes past me. "Let's watch *The Wizard of Oz*, guys!"

Running my hand over my face, I try to figure out what the fuck I'm going to do next.

"We were going to show them the tape we've been working on; how about that instead?"

Great idea, Stanley.

"But then can we watch *The Wizard of Oz*? It's my favorite movie of all time. And it has to be the original. The original is the best. I can show you all sorts of things you never even noticed in the film, because I used to watch it every day. It's the best movie ever."

"Ever?" Blade asks, fucking with her.

I walk into the room and lean against the wall, watching Bella walk in a circle and smile at everyone.

"Oh yes, it is. The absolute best." She turns and looks at Maze. "Maze, I think you'll love it most of all."

"I've seen it."

She lunges at him and hugs him. "Isn't it the best movie in the ...?" She stops midsentence, lifts her nose in the air, and sniffs. "Pizza!"

She looks at Axel. "Pizza's the best food on the planet. Pizza in Italy is so different than in Jersey." She scratches her head. "Actually, different than pizza in New York, too. And they call themselves Italians." She slaps her knee and snorts. "*Folle.*"

"What?" Ranger chuckles.

She spins in a circle and grins when her eyes land on him. "*Folle*. It means *crazy* in Italian."

"You speak Italian?"

"No, Momma Joe does. She's from there. Her mother is Isabella, and that's who I was named after, which makes no sense because Momma Joe left there at seventeen and married my grandpa Jonathon. He died. I never got to meet him. It makes me sad, Ranger." She grabs his hand. "Really, really sad because he was alive, and my mom's parents had custody, and they never let me see them. I didn't meet my father until I was seven." She lifts her nose in the air, drops his hand, and sniffs again. "Pizza. God, I'm hungry. Shit, it's because of the cannabis bears, right? Or did I not eat today? Oh fuck." She turns toward Axel. "It's short-term memory loss, right? That's what happens, and it's already happening, and I really don't want it to happen. I have some amazing memories from the past month, and I don't want to forget them. Fuck." She walks over and sits on the bed. "Next thing you know, I'll be buying Sweet Leaf jewelry and screaming, *fuck the police!*" Which she literally screams. "God, I want to learn Italian. How do you think you'd say fuck the police and Sweet Leaf in Italian? God, I want to learn Italian."

I grab a box off the top of the pile of pizzas and walk over, sitting next to her and opening the box. "How about you try some pizza made by an Italian—Little Caesar."

"Caesar would roll over in his tomb. He wasn't Italian; he was Roman." She grins at me then gives me a wink.

Here we fucking go, I think to myself.

Then it's as if her mind snaps its fingers in front of her.

"Actually, he was cremated. What they call his tomb is on the ruins of the Temple of Caesar, and it looks like a big pile of elephant shit. You wanna see a tomb, Tags? You should see Napoleon's in Paris. King Tut would roll over in his sarcophagus." She stops and looks at Grimm. "You would totally love it."

"Is it six feet under? If so, no thank you; that's a lot of work just to see a dead thing."

She pouts out her bottom lip. "I love you, Grimm." She crawls up the bed and musses up his hair. "Both parts of you."

"I love you, too, Little Bellarina."

She laughs out loud and from her belly. "Oh my God, I hated ballet class. I used to beg Dad to let me stay with him at the shop instead of going, but he was all like"—she clears her throat then talks in what I assume she thinks her father sounds like—"*Little Bell, you made a commitment, and we Steels stick to our commitments*. I would've liked to see him dancing around to a bunch of boring piano music with a bunch of stuffy-ass bitches." She sniffs the air again. "Tags, pizza."

"How long does this shit last?" Breaker asks.

"Any of you know the number to wherever the fuck you bought the shit?" I ask.

"Edible truck on the strip. Blazed Goods," Axel answers.

"Hey." Bella pokes me. "Are you gonna sit there with all that yummy goodness on your lap, or are you gonna put it in my mouth?"

Pins dropping from a mile away could be heard, and she hasn't a fucking clue.

She pokes me again then takes the pizza. "Fine by me. I'll eat it all by myself and lick my fingers clean afterward. No piece of pizza for you tonight, Tag-a-lag-a-ding-dong."

"Holy fucking shit, man, you gonna do something about

that, or you gonna sit there like a rabid dog waiting for the chain to get cut loose?" Blade laughs.

I glare at him. "She's fucked up, sayin' shit she doesn't even know she's sayin', so you back the fuck off her."

"I know exactly what I'm sayin'." She takes a bite of the pizza then smiles. "It may only be half-Italian, but it tastes like sexy goodness to—"

"Someone put on the movie," I cut her off.

"We're kind of enjoying the pizza porn, man. No harm, no foul." Axel smirks.

"Stanley?" I nearly beg.

An hour later, and she's balled up in bed, crying as we watch the movie.

"I love you all so much. We're family, right?"

Maze chuckles. "You getting any of this on tape, Stan?"

"Wouldn't be right to tape her when she didn't know it."

Something about the way he says it has me thinking he's full of shit.

I glance toward the TV stand and see the little camera sitting there.

"Stan, Maze, why are you over there and not with the crew?" Bella sniffles.

Can't believe I'm about to say this, but I do. "Your little leader has called; you should go."

As soon as they do, and when no one's looking, I snatch the camera and go into the bathroom. I pull out the SD card and pocket it.

Fucker, I think as I walk back out, camera hidden behind me, and place it back where it was.

"I'm so thirsty." She wipes her tears.

I hate tears, but it's not from pain or sorrow; it's canna-bear induced.

* * *

"CAN WE WATCH IT AGAIN? Please, please, please. I promise it's different every time." Swear to God, she's taken on the pouty tone of Dorothy's voice.

I look over at her. Her eyes are closed, and we're twenty minutes in.

I look around her. All eyes are glued to the TV. This is what Stan should have taped. Fucking comical. A bed full of stoned badasses watching a movie and eating everything in sight.

"How long did the guy say before the high wore off?" Blade asks.

"Few hours, maybe longer." Maze answers still looking at the TV.

Blade shakes his head, "It's been three, man, and as comical as it's been, I think I'm gonna jet. You wanna hang?"

I shake my head. "Thanks, though. Maybe next time."

Blade gives me his fist. "Catch you tomorrow."

I look at my watch. Half an hour before Luna calls.

"I'm heading out, too." Breaker pats my back. "Have fun with the crew."

I nod. "Yeah."

"Should have eaten the shit they all did." He laughs as he walks out.

Five high as fuck men and her all on the bed. She looks ... well, she's drooling. Still looks good, though.

I walk over to the bed. "How you feeling, Grimm?"

"Fucking beautiful." He smiles as he looks at the TV.

"I'm gonna get this one to her room."

"She can stay," Ranger, who's acting as a foot stool for the little stoner, says.

"You guys need to get ready for his date. Chaperone if necessary."

"A hooker." He grins. "Paid for extras, too."

"Yeah, so we've heard ... five times, man. Have fun. Wrap that shit."

I lift Bella over my shoulder and walk toward the door.

"Hey," she mumbles. "No fair. I was partying like a fucking rock star, buddy."

Thankfully, the door shuts behind me before she grabs two handfuls of my ass.

"Easy, sweets. Go back to sleep."

She laughs and swats my ass hard enough that it stings. "Imma bite your ass."

"You do, and I'll spank yours."

Bad fucking thing to say. She bites my back instead.

"Isabella, I will wreck your ass if you do that shit again."

"If you're going to be a douche, take me back to my boys."

"You're done for the night, girl." I laugh as I slide the key card in the slot.

"I'll scream for help if you don't take me back. I'm not ready yet."

"I'm calling it a night for you."

"Let me go!" she screams then laughs.

As soon as I flop her ass on the bed, I'm pushed from behind and into the fucking wall.

"You have two seconds to take your hands off me before I ..." I stop when my arm gets wrenched back.

Panic sets in.

"Bella, get the fuck out of here!"

I fight with all I am to turn the fuck around, giving myself a fair chance at two on one.

When I get turned, I realize it's not two; it's four.

"Um, Carter?"

"Bella, I said get the fuck out NOW!"

"Bella, you keep your ass put and call a fucking ambulance before you call security. No one puts their hands on my little girl."

Same coloring, similar features.

Fuck me, I think as I release his shirt.

"You must be Bella's father."

He pushes his forearm into my chest, his glare intensifying.

"I think you've got the wrong impression, and I also think you better take your hands off me before I decide to fight back, and that won't be good for either one of us."

"You feeling froggy, boy? Jump."

"Jase!" A woman with blonde hair gets between us.

"Not now, C. I'm kind of busy."

"I will wring your neck if you don't let the young man go, Steel."

His head takes a hard left as he looks at her like she's nuts. "Don't pull this now."

"I can fight, Jase. I can fight and scratch and—"

"Baby, you didn't even bring your vagina hat, so simmer down and let me take care of this shit."

"I don't need a vagina hat; I have a crown and stilettos." She glares back at him, and he smiles at her. She shakes her head as she tries not to smile. "Let go of him and go say hi to your daughter."

He's loosened up enough that I quickly slide out from under him and past three other sets of glaring eyes.

"Everything good in here?" Maze pops his head in.

"Everything's good." I nod as I try to block his view of the shitstorm beyond me.

"You wanna go with us? I paid for extra. Whatever extra is," Grimm says from behind Maze.

"Dude, no one wants to share a hooker with you, Grimm." Ranger laughs. "She's all yours, stud."

Ranger attempts to walk past me, but I block him.

"Oh yeah, you with the good intentions, taking blazed Bella back to her room."

"Bella, you got water in here? Cottonmouth is killing me right now." Axel stands toe-to-toe with me. "Dude, you do not want to stand between me and water right now. I will throw down."

"Lots of water in here," another woman's voice says from behind me. "Come on in; we'd love to meet y'all."

"Well, baby doll, we'd love to be met." Ranger grins over my shoulder at her. "Hey y'all, I'm Ranger."

"Baby doll has an angry daddy, Ranger dick; you may want to show some fucking respect."

"Zandor," she scolds.

"Kitten," he says softly but with command, "not now. I'm full of my twenty-year-old's testosterone and the top floor's pretty fucking far away."

Another woman giggles. "Oh, come on. They're Bella's friends." She ducks under my arm.

"Birdy," another voice warns.

"I'm Tara." She sticks her hand out. "Nice to meet you."

"You hear that, boys?" Another male laughs. "That's the sound of your balls being deflated when you find one worth keeping."

"Nice, Xavier." Yet another woman laughs.

I look back as the redhead high-fives who I now know is Xavier.

"I have a good idea." Bella finally decides to show up.

"How about we watch *The Wizard of Oz* again? I really like that movie."

Axel, Maze, Ranger, and Grimm all say, "We know; it's your favorite."

I step back, and they all pile in.

I look over as Bella gives her father a smile. "Daddy, this is Axel, Maze, Grimm, Ranger, and Tags. Guys, this is my dad, Momma Carly, Cyrus, Tara, Zandor, Bekah, Xavier, and Taelyn, my aunts and uncles."

She looks back at Jase. "Dad, I'm high as fuck, so if this is you and not a hallucination caused by canna-bears, you're gonna have to excuse me while I drink a gallon of water and fall asleep for a while."

Jase looks at me and points. "You care to explain?"

My phone vibrates in my pocket. "Sure. After I talk to my daughter."

As I'm walking out, I hear Maze say, "It's actually a pretty funny story."

"Yeah? You think my daughter being high is fucking funny, man?"

Bella yawns. "Imaginary Daddy, be nice to him; he's Forever Steel."

"Do I look imaginary, Isabella?" he snaps.

"I sure hope so because, if not, you're going to be so pissed at me."

"Bella ..." Jase groans.

When she doesn't answer, I assume she's passed out.

Lucky girl.

I step out into the hallway and look at the phone. She doesn't normally FaceTime at night. I hit *accept*.

"Hey, baby girl. What color's the sky?"

"Pink and yellow."

"Pink and yellow, huh?"

"What color's yours?" she asks.

I look up. "I'm inside, but remember, we have a time difference now."

She nods. "How many more sleeps?"

I hold up two fingers, and she grins.

"You sleepy, baby girl?"

She nods and rubs her eyes.

"Time to put the moon to sleep?"

"Then send it to you?"

"You're in charge of the moon, Luna. You tell me."

"The moon's tired."

"Then the moon should go to sleep."

"You going to sleep?"

"As soon as the moon gets here."

"Love you, Daddy."

"Love you, too, Luna. Give the old lady a hug goodnight."

"Face phone in the morning?"

"Every morning till I see you again."

"I get a puppy when we win." She yawns.

"Yeah, baby girl, you get a puppy when we win. Love you, Luna."

"Love you, Daddy." She leans in and looks closer at me. "Hey, Daddy, who's the pretty lady?"

I look behind me as Carly waves.

"A friend, Luna."

"She gonna be my mommy?"

Carly laughs. "Sweet girl, I am too old to be your mommy."

Luna sighs and frowns. "Well, okay."

"When you get one, she's sure gonna be a lucky woman."

Luna's face lights up. "Well, I hope I get a puppy first."

Carly laughs. "Yeah?"

Luna grins. "A big, fluffy one."

"I'm sure all your dreams will come true." She holds up an ice bucket. "It was nice chatting with you, Luna. I have to go get some water. My little girl is thirsty."

"What's her name?"

Carly looks at me then back at Luna. "Her name is Bella."

"Like on the movie with the beast?"

"But a little more real."

TWENTY

MEET THE FAMILY

TAGS

I end the call with my girl and see Carly leaning against the wall across the hall.

"You need help getting ice?"

She nods, pushes herself off the wall, and says, "Sure."

"It's just down here," I say as I walk toward her and take the ice bucket. "How's Isabella?"

"Well"—she half-laughs—"she's either passed out or pretending to be."

"The guys still alive?"

"Mine or yours?" she asks.

I laugh.

She smiles. "They're fine."

"Good. Bad timing. She didn't mean to eat those things."

"You partake?" she asks.

"Not this trip," I tell her honestly. "Not gonna say I never have, but it's been awhile."

"About four years?" she asks.

"Would make me more likeable to say yes, but no."

"I don't think you're unlikable, but my husband, well,

he heard you tell who we weren't sure was Bella or not at the moment that she was done for the night. Then, well, you know the rest of the conversation. That led him to believe there was something fishy going on. He didn't see the man with the cute little girl, so I'll apologize for him."

I hold the bucket under the ice maker and push it against the release. When it's filled up, I turn toward her.

"But if I were you, I'd be real with him."

I swallow hard. "About what?"

She shakes her head. "Anything and everything. He'll flip shit, then he'll chill."

"He'll flip shit on a grown man?"

"Um, *hello*, but was that you against the wall?" She laughs.

I nod. "True, but he thought I was going to hurt Bella, so I get it. The thing is, I never will."

She'll be the one to fuck me up, I think.

"Why would she fuck you up?"

"There are times, like just then, I think shit and don't mean to say it. Could you do me a favor and forget I said that?"

She shakes her head.

"I didn't think so."

"Spill it."

I lean against the wall next to the door. "She's special, beautiful, real, says whatever she wants, kind to men like me and all the others. She's not been really hard to fall for. The problem is, my life's complicated right now. When I met her, I said see you in six to nine months. Then she shows up."

"Wait. You already knew her?"

I nod.

"From school?"

I shake my head.

"Well, how?"

"Same way I know you're love."

She covers her mouth and looks pretty fucking horrified. "Oh God, please forgive me for this but, if her dad finds out, he's gonna hurt you."

I shrug. "Wouldn't ask you to lie to your husband. I will ask you to do what's best for Bella. I certainly plan to."

The door opens, and the guys all walk out.

"You sure you don't want to go—"

"Grimm, dude, have fun." I half-laugh.

I hold the door for Carly. "After you."

When we walk in, Bella is sitting up and leaning against the uncle with the least attitude. Xavier, I think.

I set the ice down, and she looks up. A goofy-ass grin spreads across her face.

"Still not feeling straight?"

"Look around, Tags. Right now, I'm wishing I had more of those gummies."

She's serious as shit. She's also acting like they aren't even here.

Xavier laughs. "Me, too, Little Bell."

"Xavier," his wife scolds him.

"Irish, we have a teenage boy; been straight for way too many years. We're in Vegas, Momma Joe has the kids; let's eat some fucking gummies."

Bella laughs, and Jase growls.

"Daddy ..." she sighs, "you do know that I am a twenty-three-year-old woman, right?"

"You do know that I'm your father, right?"

"Oh yes, and so does every boy I dated in college. Hell, your picture was sent from one asshole to the next with a warning."

"Good," he huffs.

"Not gonna say I disagree. None were worth a damn anyway."

"What the fuck is that supposed to mean?" he snaps.

And I find myself siding with her father.

She peeks up at me, bloodshot eyes through thick lashes, and shakes her head.

"Bella, I asked you a question," he demands.

"Then you'll get an answer you won't like, but you'll get it. Then I'm gonna go to sleep, because I ate some gummies that I didn't know were ..." She looks at me and smiles. "What did you call them?"

I narrow my eyes. "Canna-bears."

"This asshole give them to you?"

She whips her head around and scowls at him. "This asshole ..." She looks back at me and cringes. "Sorry."

"It's all good." I nod.

She turns back to him. "He didn't, and neither did the others. I saw candy in a fridge after I sat at that desk and edited a film that I'll never be able to use because his wife hates me."

Xavier breathes out, "Fuuuuck." And four women stand in front of me.

"The hell are you all doing?" Jase asks.

Fucker looks crazy, like seriously crazy. Like he's the bull, and I'm the asshole with the red flag kind of crazy.

"They know how you are. They're protecting the man who I am falling in love with—"

"You're what?"

I do him a solid and keep my face unreadable, when inside, my heart is doing all kinds of shit. It's a fucking party in there. A big fucking party. Looking around, I realize it's the equivalent to someone finding out they won the lottery at a funeral of someone they don't know but are attending to support a friend.

She looks at me. "Have I said that yet tonight?"

"Not tonight. Not in the past month. Not at all actually."

Carly whips around and looks horrified.

I look at Jase as he looks between us, back and forth, back and forth, like a pendulum swinging as a countdown commences, before the bomb goes off.

"She doesn't know about us," Bella says.

This poor man is getting it from all sides.

"It's a long story."

"Can you tell it in the next ten seconds? Because you got about that long before I lose my shit all over you."

I force a smile. "I'm doing this for her, not you."

"You don't have to." Isabella starts to stand up then falls on her ass.

"Pretty sure I'll do a better job than you right now."

I look at Jase. "She needs me to explain myself, because you need answers. You need answers because you love her. That's the only reason I'm putting my ass on the line, and when I say I'm putting my ass on the line, it should come with the realization that I know what you went through to get Isabella back in your life. I don't want to be in the same boat ever. You may not respect me, but it's not you I'm truly concerned with."

He doesn't like that much. He loves his daughter, he'll adjust.

"Left home when I was sixteen. Wasn't a good home. Got arrested for some stupid shit, went to juvy, and met some new friends. Got out and didn't go home again. They never looked, still don't look, and I don't care. Joined a gang, had a threesome, got the girl pregnant. Yes, I know she's mine. Before she found out she was knocked up, she and the other guy—"

"Neo," Bella interrupts.

I nod. "They became a thing. I had no interest in her that way, so it was easy. He found out she was pregnant; she was too far along to do shit about it. Baby came out my color, not his. She said she wanted to get married. I was already in it for life with a kid—I could have made it work—so I was down."

"Then she left him and Luna when she was an infant, and they were homeless, and an old lady took them in," Bella finishes.

"You missed a part. She made me turn myself in for all the warrants—vandalism. Well, graffiti. She took care of my girl, and when I got out, she had a job lined up for me. She's the one who pushed me to do this, and I'm going to win so I can make sure she's taken care of like she took care of us."

Jase still looks pissed. The others don't. Either way, I don't care.

As a father, the next part is what would bother me, so I'm ready for whatever.

"The extra push was when I found out who Mara really was."

Bella interrupts, "When he was trying to get her to sign papers for their divorce."

"She's David, the executive producers, daughter. She's a spoiled, little, rich bitch who's had no type of supervision. Her dad doesn't know about Luna, or about me. She's avoided me all she can, but I have papers for her to sign. My only fear is David will get wind of it and go after some sort of custody for Mara. She's not mother material, and she isn't gonna fuck my girl up. If I could avoid the shit for the rest of my life, I would. But I'm twenty-three years old and my girl deserves better. I'm the only one who's gonna make that happen. Just got something to deal with first."

"She's freaking crazy, too. Hates me. So, she can't know about him and me. She'd avoid signing to spite me."

"Or tell her father about my girl. I don't have David's money. I might never. Doesn't mean I'm not good enough for her. I know damn well I'm the best she'll ever have."

"You do that to my girl's back?" Jase asks.

"Still working on some of my issues."

He huffs, "She ends up ditching you—and odds are, she will—the next man that she's with—"

"The next man who bends her over will see she's taken."

Carly whispers, "No, nope, nuh-uh, not something I'd—"

"You and I need to take a walk." Jase's eyes are an interesting shade of amber.

This is gonna suck.

I push myself off the wall, and Bella jumps up.

"No!" She points at him then at me. "Please don't do this."

Jase sneers, "How the hell does he get a please and I get a no?"

I smile at her. "She's already got your love, and she's just realized she's falling in love with me." I look up at the man whose eyes are murderous. "I'm assuming that will change when she hears those words from me."

"Might wanna say 'em now. Pretty sure he's gonna bust your jaw." Cyrus laughs tauntingly.

"You want me to get a picture of the two of you before his face is fucked up, Little Bell?" Zancor's laugh is lighter, but he seems serious to me.

"Just go with it, man. No one wants to fight someone who's not fighting back." Xavier's suggestion.

I lean down, eyes on her father, and brush my lips across her forehead. "I'll be back in a little while."

"No!"

I cock my head to the side, lean in, and whisper, "We have two nights left here; you really want to *deny* me the right to get this out of the way?"

She leans in and whispers to me, "I like your lips; don't let him bust them."

I smile as I step back. "See you later."

"Yes, you will." But she doesn't say those words to me; she says them to her father.

I step out first, and he follows.

"Would like to do this in private? The hall's full of cast, crew, and I'm assuming Mara."

"You think I give a fuck?"

"Yeah, actually, I do."

He doesn't respond as he follows me down the hall.

Once I open my door, I see some of her shit laying around. When I turn around, he swings.

I don't block, and I don't move. I let him hit me.

"You got nothing to say?" he snaps.

I shrug. "Nothing you wanna hear."

He swings again. This time I grab his fist.

"Ask me what I did for money to eat from ages sixteen to eighteen?"

"Don't give a fuck."

I shove his hand away. "Fought. I'm pretty fucking quick. Ask me why?"

He swings again, and I catch it and shove it away again.

"Because I learned real quick how to avoid shit flying at

me from a deranged mother from the time I was old enough to remember shit."

"You expect me to feel sorry for you?"

"Not my point. My point is, she'll be loved, she'll be protected, she'll be looked after."

"Like she is here!"

"Not an answer you wanna hear, but yeah, she's been well looked after."

"You're damn right it's not something I wanna hear." His jaw muscles tense.

"The guys on team Bella love that girl. She's looked after even when I'm not around. That better?"

"The ones who allowed her to eat fucking edibles?"

"That was a fluke."

"So you're telling me she works, and then you suck every bit of time out of her!"

"No, she does whatever she wants to do. I just make sure I'm around."

"So you're obsessed with my daughter!"

"With all due respect, it seems like nothing I say is gonna make you happy, so why—"

"Exactly."

"Wasn't gonna say why bother. I was gonna say why fight it."

"You want your daughter with some man who ..." He stops.

"Right now, yeah. In twenty years, I'm not sure how I'll feel. But when I get there, I'll look back on this moment right here."

He looks between my eyes, trying to read me.

"You think I'm full of shit? Some punk who just wants a good piece of ass? I can assure you that's not the case. Something sparked when we met. Something I've never felt. And even though I haven't said the words to your daughter, and I'm not about to tonight, I loved her the minute I saw her. I will love her until she tells me to fuck off. And I will bust my ass to make sure that never happens. And if you think love at first sight is a joke, man"—I sigh—"I'm sorry because it's not just a game changer; it changes your heart's rhythm."

Silence, and then I laugh. "Isabella, I can feel you from here."

Jase begins, "You're fucking cra—"

"I'm pissed at you for hitting him," she spews as she hurries into view.

"You're not alone." Carly walks in and, yeah, the rest follow her.

"Your lip's bleeding." She runs her thumb over it. "Come on; let's clean it up."

TWENTY-ONE
HE LOVES ME

BELLA

As soon as we're in the bathroom, I shut the door behind me. "I'm so sor—"

He kisses me hard, running his hands up my back. With one, he pulls me closer, and then grips the back of my skull with the other.

I taste him, and copper, and him. When he pulls back, taking my lip with him, his eyes are different. They smolder.

I finish my sentiment, "ry."

"You feel better?"

"You're asking me if I feel better when my ASSHOLE father just punched you?"

"Prolly gonna hit a few boys, too, Bella. I get it; he's being protective. He loves you."

"And you love me."

He smirks. "I like you a whole lot."

"I heard you say it to my father."

"Yeah, pretty fucked-up kind of confessional we got going here."

"Carter ..."

He kisses me again, this time harder, and then he pulls

away quicker. "Fuck." He turns around and takes a few deep breaths. "You gotta give me a couple minutes to get my shit straight. Make that *less straight.*"

I laugh. "Such a waste of a perfectly good—"

Bang, bang, bang!

"Doesn't take that long to clean up a scratch, Isabella."

"Your father?" He jokes.

"Is that who that is?" I act all surprised.

"Go. Give me a minute."

"I'll give you whatever you want."

"Not helping the situation, Isabella. Get the hell out of here."

Laughing, I walk out the door and shut it behind me. I look around. It's just Dad and Carly. Not good.

"Where'd they go?"

"They went to get ready for dinner. We have reservations. You should go get ready, too."

"I'm not going anywhere like this." I shake my head.

"You can get cleaned up. We'll wait."

I look at him like he's crazy, because he is. "I may still be a bit buzzed, but I'm not leaving you alone in here."

Tags walks out. "Bella, I'm fine. Go have fun with your family."

"But—"

"Go," he insists.

I walk over and grab my dad's hand. "Let's go."

"I'm gonna wait here until you're ready."

"No, you're not."

"Yes, I am."

"Isabella," Tags says on a sigh. "It's fine. He and I will be fine."

Dad mumbles, "One of us will be."

"Jase Steel, I will —"

"Carly Steel," he cuts her off, "you will go help Bella get ready and take her pile of shit with you. Then you will—"

"You mind if I stay with you tonight?" Carly asks me. "Your father has lost his damn mind. Maybe we should find those gummies, give him a couple to help him relax, and maybe then he'll be able to see past the wall he's built in front of you. See that you look happy. See the little birdies chasing hearts in a halo pattern around your head."

Dad sighs. "C, baby, please just—"

"I remember that feeling. Do you, Jase?"

She hooks my arm in hers and swipes a pile of clothes off the bed. I cringe when I see the underwear,

"Those are clean," Tags tells her, and we both turn around. "You had shit to do. I was doing a load anyway."

"That is very thoughtful of you," Carly says as a dig to Dad.

"Thanks. I'll do yours next time."

He gives me a millisecond wink, and I smile with my whole heart.

Once in my room, Carly tosses my stuff on the bed then wraps me in a big hug. "He's beautiful."

I laugh and hug her back. "And he loves me."

She steps back, holding my shoulders. "Like crazy. And I know this might be weird, but I know that look. It's—"

I don't know why, but I start to cry.

"Little Bell, what is wrong?"

"I've waited a whole lifetime to have a man look at me that way, to talk to me that way, to make me feel the way he does. I never thought I would. I thought maybe you and Dad had something that only happens once in a blue moon. But you see it, right?"

"I don't just see it; I feel it."

"Then why are you frowning?"

"It's a difficult situation. No one wants to see their daughter go through what the two of you may face. Hell, you're already facing it. You have to hide so he can get this woman to sign papers?"

"Kat on steroids," I tell her.

She cringes. "Well, maybe she'll find a Ricco."

"Yeah, well, then what? Then she gets her life together and tries to get Luna? Which would be fine, you know, visitation. But apparently, she's been in and out of rehab several times. And even if she got sober, she is a vile human being. No child deserves that."

"What does he say about it?"

"Well, we don't really talk about it much."

She sucks in a breath. "The two of you need to."

"We're a month in; that's pretty heavy."

"You love him, Bella, and love makes all things possible."

TWENTY-TWO

TWO DADS

TAGS

"I'd say sorry about the lip, but I'm not and we deal in truths in this family."

"I can appreciate that." I lean back against the wall.

"Then give me some."

"Ask anything you want."

"You're hell-bent on this divorce; have you even thought about custody? That's a whole different matter."

"One step at a time."

"Custody should be your first step."

"I get that you think I'm some dumb-ass punk, but I'm not. And you'll take this and run with it like a wildfire in California, but I know how to manipulate and maneuver, and I know Mara. I'm doing this the way it needs to be done."

"So, a divorce; how's that been handled the past couple months you've been around her?"

"She's got to be served. When I find someone to do it, without the circus around us knowing, she'll be served."

"How you gonna find some random person to serve her?"

"As I said, I know how to manipulate and maneuver. I'll know if I can trust someone."

He pushes off the wall opposite me. "Cyrus has taken care of getting her served."

"Excuse me?" I ask.

"He knows people. She's gonna get served, and you'll be divorced if she doesn't contest it within a month. Then what?"

"You do know the minute she sees all of you out to dinner with Bella, she'll connect the fucking dots, and that puts a target on her."

"Right, but you're not dealing with idiots. We're not doing the serving. It's being handled by someone who knows how to handle shit. You could have hired a fucking cop to do it, Tags."

"I'm not one to pay for shit I can get handled for free. But if you paid some cop, I want to know how much."

He smirks and shakes his head. "Don't always have to pay people. Some of us still do the right thing for our friends without greasing a palm."

"So, who is it I owe a favor?"

"Me, Cyrus, and his old Navy buddy Tank who works security at Hard Rock."

"Sometimes, it's easier to pay one person than owe three."

"That would cheapen the favor."

"I don't do favors."

He looks down. "We'll see."

"Okay, I've entertained your need to protect the virtue of your twenty-three-year-old daughter, but you're overstepping."

"Me and my brothers don't overstep; we play whack-a-mole with issues. One pops up, one of us smashes it, and we get excited about the next. That girl thinks she loves you; you'll have to learn how to deal with it."

"I'm not sure I like you."

He starts laughing like I'm joking. I'm not.

"Say that to her once, and you'll be ejected like a pilot from a bad plane."

I lift my chin.

He lifts his then pushes off the wall. "Well, it's been one hell of a time. I'd ask you to join us, but you can't. Secrets and shit."

"You say it like it's an option. I'm keeping secrets for her safety and for my daughter's future."

"You got a custody lawyer?"

"I have custody of my daughter. Legal custody. Uncontested."

He looks back at me. "You might want to lawyer up, son. If she's as bad as you make her out to be, she'll try to fuck shit up."

Did he just call me son?

"My bad."

I'm saying shit out loud to him now? What the fuck!

He opens the door.

"Hey."

He turns back.

"You make damn sure she's safe."

"You backing out now?"

I narrow my eyes. "Not a fucking chance."

He purses his lips, and then his eyes smile. How do I know? She has the same eyes, just a different color.

I got your tell, Poppa Steel. I got your tell.

I grab my phone out of my pocket and send her a text.

Me: *Have a good time with your family. See you in the morning. And hey, I like you a lot. ~ Tags*

Bella: *I'm not sleeping alone. I'll text after I've tucked the 'rents in for the night. And hey, I know. ~ B.S.*

I'd love to close my eyes and take a power nap, but adrenaline is coursing through my body like never before. So, I decide to hit the hotel gym.

* * *

AFTER TWO HOURS, my body is exhausted, and because of the endorphins floating around in there, my head's in a better place.

Inside the elevator, I order room service, needing to fuel the bod in order to fuck her the way she likes to be fucked. Or maybe try to make love to her. Always thought there was a difference. I fucked her to own her, but she fucked me right back.

Stepping off the elevator, I walk down the hall, looking at my phone. When I see shoes of the very expensive sort, I look up.

"Do you have a minute?"

It's David.

I nod. "Sure."

"You mind if we talk inside? I don't need the entire floor knowing I stopped by."

I slide my key over the sensor then open the door. "Come on in."

As soon as the door shuts, he pulls a file out of the inside of his jacket and tosses it onto the bed.

"What's that?"

"Four and a half years' worth of my daughter's life."

My fists clench at my sides.

He unbuttons his coat, takes it off, slings it over the back of the desk chair, and then sits. Pointing to it, he says, "Go ahead. See for yourself."

"Don't need to see shit. What do you want?"

"Same thing I've been asking myself about you for the past few months." He leans back and crosses one leg over the other. "Why is a lowlife PI looking into my daughter and myself?"

"Digs is a good man."

"You pay for what you get, I suppose."

My blood starts pumping harder. "Good isn't bought and paid for and bad isn't born; it's created."

"So Mara's shortcomings are because of me?" He points to himself.

"I'm not pointing fingers, just connecting dots."

"You hire a man like Digger, with a low budget to work with, and the surface is scratched. With money, you can buy more information."

"Good to know, but I'm having a hard time trying to open my mind up to your lesson when I have yet to figure out your intentions."

"I'm giving you ten thousand dollars' worth of information for free, yet you don't seem to even want to look."

"Don't remember wanting ten thousand dollars' worth of shit from you, so why don't you just let me know what you really want?"

"I want a sick little girl to be healthy."

"Luna is none of your concern."

"I'm talking about Mara. There're things you should know about her, and then maybe could walk away from the game you're playing with her so she can focus on healing."

"I'm not playing a fucking game. I just wanted to find the woman I married—at her insistence—and then bailed so I can move the fuck on with my life."

He leans forward. "You sure that's it?"

"Do I look like I have shit to lose from lying?"

"I'm sure that may have been how it started, but once you found out she was wealthy, you made some moves that are telling me otherwise. Like coming here."

"So I could get her served and win this little contest so I can give back to the woman who took us in."

"I just left her room. She's been served. So, why are you still here, if not for money?"

"I don't take what I don't earn. I'll win your contest, because I'm the best artist you have."

The fucker shakes his head and looks at me like I'm some pathetic lowlife.

"She didn't want the baby."

Pissed at how he references the sole reason I've become who I am, I slam back. "And I never wanted yours."

"I'm aware of the events of the night she was conceived. I didn't even have to pay for that information. The question still remains: what do you want from her?"

"I want nothing but a promise that this is over and that she's not going to ever try to fuck up the masterpiece I've created for my daughter about how she became."

"Care to share that information?"

A knock on the door has my stomach immediately in knots. He doesn't know about Bella, and he can't.

"Open the fucking door, Tags!"

"Jesus Christ." David sighs as he stands.

"Right fucking now!"

David whips the door open.

"What the fuck are you doing here?"

"The question is: what are *you* doing here?"

"Oh, please, David." She pushes past him. "I've been

cheeking pills since Mom died and you started drugging me."

She storms over to me and thrusts the papers at my chest. "You got what you wanted. Happy?"

"You weren't easy to find, Mara, so I guess I am." I take the envelope and open it to make sure she's signed them properly.

"They're signed. Now what? You gonna try to make me be a mom again?"

"Wasn't really something forced on you; it happened."

"And now I have a kid who's gonna pop up someday and try to get me to feel bad that I walked. Well, I don't. I tried to make her go away. You gonna tell her that? That her issues are a botched home abortion?"

"No, I'm—"

"You should have let me die!" she cries. "You should have let her die, but you didn't, and now I'm always going to be looking over my shoulder, and she's always going to wonder why the woman who gave birth to her doesn't want her. I hate you! I hate you so fucking much!" She slams her fist against my chest as tears begin to fall. "I'd kill you with my bare hands if I didn't know she'd come looking for me!"

"You wanna know what she thinks, Mara?"

"I don't want anything from her. I wish she had died!" she screams, covering her belly with her hands. "I wish my baby had died."

The pain in her voice contradicts the words she's spewing. Out of instinct, I reach out to comfort her.

"Don't you touch me!" She fists my shirt. "Don't you act like you understand!" She leans her head against my chest. "You have no idea what it's like to be me."

"Never said I did, Mara. Never were all that easy to figure out either. You have a wall—"

"She has a mental health issue. She has a disease. She's two people in one body. Just like her mother was," David says with no sort of emotion. "But she's going to be okay. I'm going to make sure of it." He reaches into his pocket and hands me three pills. "She needs these."

"They make me feel like shit."

I look at him, his eyes.

"They keep you here, Mara."

Bang, bang, bang!

"She's in there, Tags, I'm gonna rip your nuts out through your throat."

David walks over and opens the door.

"Sorry, man. Is Mara here?"

I look down at Mara, and she looks up, searching my eyes. Then she steps back. Hers are softer, like Luna's, but then they're hard again.

"What the fuck do you want, Neo?" she snaps.

"You stashed these, and you need them"—he points to me—" 'cause he's here. 'Cause he's throwing shit in your face."

"Neo." David's voice isn't as calm as normal.

"He goes this week."

"And you go now." David points to the door.

"Mara." Neo gives her pleading eyes.

"I'll catch up with you later."

"Take the pills," he nearly begs before leaving.

I hold them out, and she looks at me. "You need 'em, Mara, you should take them."

"Does she need them?"

"Luna?" I shake my head.

"Mara didn't until eighteen," David says.

Her nose scrunches as she closes her eyes.

"I'll make sure to keep an eye on it," I tell David.

Mara opens her eyes and looks up. "She still scream all the time?"

I'm tempted to tell her that Luna is a fucking nightmare, just to keep her away, but it's fucking wrong.

"Nah, she's good. Really good."

"Her arm?"

"Her lucky fin."

"What?" she asks.

"The movie, *Finding Nemo*. I told her she was like him—had a lucky fin. She's had a couple surgeries. Only two-inch difference. Not noticeable."

"Has she asked ...?" She doesn't finish the sentence.

I nod. "She's in an early ed program. Came home asking who her mom was."

She shakes her head.

"I hated you for a long time, Mara. Didn't understand how you could beg me to marry you then take off when I was letting you nap while taking Luna for a walk. Told the doorman we weren't allowed back in, shut off my phone, and—"

"I know! I was there!"

"Okay, that's enough." David walks over.

I ignore him. "When my head was straight, I didn't hate you. I felt sorry for you that you were missing out on all the firsts."

"She doesn't deserve this," David snaps at me.

"Then I stopped being angry. Figured you had a drug issue; bigger than what I imagined. I met an angel. She took in a homeless teenager and a screaming infant."

"Because of me?"

"Because of acid reflux." I look at her. "All that screaming and those sleepless nights when all she needed was a change in formula."

She looks so fucking sad now.

"And when she asked about her mommy, Mara, I told her I always wanted to be a dad and that I just couldn't wait anymore, so I asked a beautiful woman if she would help me out. That the woman made my wish come true. I had a family. I had her."

"Is she beautiful?"

I nod. "Yes."

"Did her face get—"

"Only a few issues from the night you tried to ..." I look down then look back up. "You can't be part of her life."

She nods as more tears fall.

"You have to take care of yourself, Mara. Take the pills, go to therapy, stay the fuck away from drugs and alcohol."

"Stressful situations," David adds.

"I want this show, David." She shakes her head. "I need this."

I lift her chin. "You need to be healthy because, someday when she can understand you and wants to meet you, you better be healthy."

"I'll never be healthy."

"Not with that piss-poor attitude." I shake my head. "Fun killer."

She smiles but only briefly.

"The way we lived was wrong."

She looks back up at me.

"You never wanted to be a mom; I get it. But God, the universe, whatever you believe in decided she was supposed to be here, Mara. She saved me; you had a part in doing that, too. Let the idea of someday being strong enough to see what you created drive you. I promise you she's worth every hell you'll walk through just to see her smile."

She shakes her head.

"Then just get better in case you change your mind."

She looks away.

"And if you do that, you better make sure you tell her I paid you a million bucks because I knew you were the best one to give me her."

She looks up. "Why would you paint me like that? To let me disappoint her and make you look like the fucking hero?"

I shake my head and laugh. "She wanted a puppy, and I told her I couldn't afford one yet, because she cost a lot a money."

A burst of laughter escapes her, and she quickly covers her mouth with her hand.

"Kids don't understand money; had to break it down to her level."

Then she hugs me.

The next knock on the door has me really fucking nervous.

When David opens it and Bella is standing there, I see her smile fall.

"Something we can help you with?"

"Wrong room," she says then turns around and walks away.

Mara steps back and wipes her eyes. "Will she ever get a fucking clue?"

When I don't say anything, Mara locks up.

"Oh, hell no. Please do not tell me you're fucking—"

"Oh, go fuck yourself, Mayhem. Fuck him, and fuck this show you're ruining, too. I quit." Then she storms down the hall.

I smile, and Mara's eyes widen as she shakes her head back and forth. "That's a hard no."

"That's something I never thought I deserved, Mara. And I really need to go after her, so if we're done here ..."

"Go, you idiot," she groans. "Go get Sally Sunshine."

I walk toward the hall as Mara yells after me, "And hey, don't fuck up the fact she just quit. Her being gone is going to be a dream come true."

"She goes, I'm going." I head out the door.

TWENTY-THREE
THAT'S A WRAP

BELLA

Bang, bang, bang.

"Bella, open the door."

I don't say anything; I just peel off my dress, kick off my heels, and crawl into the bed I should've never gotten out of because everything sucks today, even gummy bears, and I love gummy bears.

Bang, bang, bang.

"Don't be such a pussy. Let him in."

I jump out of bed and rush to the door, fling it open and see her back. "You have something to say, Scare-vira, come say it to my face!"

She turns around.

"Honey, you're the least of my issues."

"You have no idea what I'm made of." I start to walk toward her when one big, stupid arm wraps around my waist and carries me into my room.

"Sweets, we don't act like that." He drops me onto the bed.

I sit up and push him. "Go back to your room. Go be with them."

He pulls off his shirt. "I'm fucking drained. I'm going to bed. You're coming with me. Big spoon, little spoon style."

"Like I want you in my bed, you giant asshole."

He reaches out and grabs me as I try to walk past him.

"I'm not playing, Tags. I'm done. I won't deal with—" He kisses me, and I finish my sentence against his stupid, pillow-soft lips. "—you."

He squats down. "She signed the papers. She's got some issues."

I laugh. "Really?"

"Mental health shit, Bella. She isn't gonna try to take my girl. Everything I set out to accomplish here is done."

I feel my bottom lip push out.

"And sweets, I am so fucking tired, and I know you must be, too, so can we sleep?"

"Why was she in your room?"

"To give me the papers, Bella. And you're pissing me off, because I know you know how I feel about you. Tomorrow is a month; one month ago, I had the moon and was ready to set the world on fire so she never knew it could be dark. But then the sun came into that shop, and I didn't wanna burn it down anymore, just light it up. No fighting, no second-guessing my intentions, no fucking gummies, because you're a pain in the ass and, sweets, no more pushing her buttons. I know she does it to you, babe, but please, for Luna, just ignore it."

I step back, walk around him, and climb up onto the bed.

When I feel him slide under the covers then wrap his arms around me to drag me back against him, I finally let out a breath.

"You better now?" he whispers against the back of my head.

"I think I'm still fucked up."

He laughs. "Tomorrow's a new day."

"It is. And now that she knows, you can eat breakfast with the family."

"Sounds like fun." He rolls me onto my back. "Hey, Bella?"

My pulse accelerates, and I hold my breath as I wait for him to say three words, three words that I've heard but never from the right man.

He kisses my nose. "I really like you a lot."

"Stating for the record that is the first time you've let me down in bed." I roll back to my side, and he laughs against my shoulder. "But tomorrow's a new day, he says."

He chuckles. "Tomorrow's a new day."

* * *

I HEAR feet shuffling before I open my eyes. When I inhale, I smell him, but I also smell Dad's cologne.

I roll to my side and open my eyes. Looking beside me, I see he's gone.

I sit up and look at Dad. "What did you do with him?"

"Good morning, Little Bella; how are you feeling?" Dad sits on the end of the bed. "High?"

I scoot off the bed and see Carly coming out of the bathroom.

"You're awake." She hugs me. "Your boyfriend called and asked if he could take us to breakfast."

"So, he is alive." I scowl at Dad.

He scowls back. "For now."

Carly sighs. "Jase, you are a forty-year-old man, not a twelve-year-old boy."

"I'm all man, baby. You remember last night? I was a man ... all night long."

"Oh my God, do not do this to me." I cover my ears.

"You fell asleep after one go."

He raises his eyebrows. "You sure about, that baby?"

Carly smirks then looks back at me. "Your father thinks if he talks about sex in front of you, it'll make you not want to have it."

"Well, I didn't have it last night, so—"

He jumps up. "Okay, fine! Go get ready, for fuck's sake."

* * *

WALKING INTO THE RESTAURANT, I see him freshly showered, arms bulging and veiny. Clearly, he's been to the gym this morning. For someone who hates to work out, I am definitely becoming a fan of the daily grind.

I smile as my steps quicken, walking toward him.

He stands up and holds out his hand as I get closer. Then he pulls me in and gives me a hug, kissing my cheek. "Welcome to our new day, Bella."

"Looks like a whole lot of fun."

He cups my cheeks and tilts my head back, looking in one eye then the next. "Thank God they're back. They were starting to remind me of my ex—"

I slap him in his rock-hard abs, knowing it doesn't hurt him one bit, but he plays it off like it does.

"Ouch, sweets. That hurt"—he grabs my hand and kisses my knuckles—"your hand." Then he steps back when I playfully swing again.

Laughing, he pulls out a chair. "Have a seat."

I step to sit, and Dad does instead.

"Thanks, cupcake."

Tags smiles and shoves Dad's chair in. "No problem, Daddy."

Carly and I smirk at each other.

He pulls out the chair next to Dad's. "Carly, have a seat."

"What a gentleman." She smiles, sits next to Dad, and then looks up. "Remember to keep doing things like pulling out chairs when you've been married as long as the old man and I have."

"You need me to turn up the swoon, baby, I'll turn it up so hot you can't handle it."

I watch him look at her and can't help smiling.

"Have a seat, Bella." Tags gestures for me to slide into the booth. Then he slides in beside me.

"Did you have a good workout?" I ask.

"Next time you go to the gym, I'd love to join you." Dad smiles a tight-lipped, antagonistic smile.

"What's your pleasure?" Tags asks, his eyes smiling.

Dad's jaw twitches.

"They have a beginners yoga class if you want to start out easy."

I have to look away from Dad, because I'm sure he's turning purple and steam is rolling out of his ears.

"That was a joke. You're a big dude. You have a mean right hook. You love Bella, and you hate that you think I'm gonna take her away, of that I'm gonna hurt her. Neither are true."

Dad nods.

Just over Dad's shoulder, I see David and Mara walking toward us.

"Oh, for the love of peace and tranquility," I mumble as I lift my water glass to my lips.

"I invited them."

I nearly choke on the water. "You what?"

"Trust me, sweets." As he stands, he kisses the top of my head.

"Morning, David, Mara. Thanks for joining us."

I look at Dad and Carly, who look as surprised as I do.

"Have a seat."

Once everyone is seated, Tags looks at them. "I think it would be best for the show if I'm the one who goes this week."

"What? No. No way," I tell him. "If you leave, so do I."

"We haven't met yet, but I'm Jase Steel, Isabella's father. And this is my wife Carly." Dad stands and shakes David's hand then ... hers.

"Very nice to meet you," David says, sitting back down.

He looks at Tags. "I agree."

"What the hell are you doing?"

"What's best for everyone." He shrugs.

I look at Mara, who rolls her eyes. "A real Dudley Do-Right, aren't you?"

"Don't talk to him like that," I scold her.

"We have a production meeting in an hour. Axel was the one being cut, but we also thought so was everyone else."

I'm so confused.

David continues, "Mara came up with a plan. She thought, instead of dumping the entire show, that maybe it could go in a different direction." He looks at me. "A new host." He looks at Tags. "A new producer. Mara is going to take some time off and work more on the business end with me."

Tags shakes his head. "I don't take handouts."

I reach under the table and hold his hand.

He looks at me and gives me a millisecond wink. "But thank you for the offer."

"I've worked hard to bring this together," Mara says, seeming eerily calm. "And as much as I don't want to admit it, Sally Sunshine's ideas were good. And you work best with the guys, Tags, so why not?"

Dad interjects, "I think the two of them may want to take a few minutes to think this over."

"Dad ..." I begin.

"We'd like to give you more time, but we're meeting with everyone soon and would like to give them solid information." David stands.

Mara looks at me. "This is about you and me, so tell me what issue you have with me being able to admit your direction was better than mine."

"Mara ..." Tags shakes his head.

"Mara, let's give them some time.' David pulls her chair out.

Once they leave, Dad leans in. "Are you two insane?"

Tags shakes his head. "What I came here to do is done. Thank you, by the way. As annoying as it was, it made things happen."

"And things are still happening, so why not take the bull by the horns? What's the worst that can happen?" He looks at me. "The show flops and you try again. You get sick of the hustle, you come home and work for me."

Tags looks at me. "You want to learn the trade?"

It dawns on me that we've never had that conversation, the one that starts with my family is filthy rich.

I look at Dad, and he starts laughing.

"Am I missing something?" Tags asks.

"Just about seventeen years of Bella's life." Dad continues to laugh.

"Jase," Carly whispers.

"Baby, this is gonna be fun." He just keeps on laughing.

"And what makes it so much fun?" She crosses her arms over her chest.

He looks at me. "I was this guy once, just hadn't gotten my girl back yet."

"Someone want to clue me in on what's going on?" Tags asks.

"My best childhood memories are in the shop with my family," I begin.

"Because they were your first, Little Bell."

"Then, well ..." I close my eyes. "My family has money."

He cocks his head to the side.

"Like, a lot. And he wants me to sit in an office and work the business end of things."

"Not fair, Little Bell. I told you business puts food on the table; the arts feed your soul."

"Tags?" Carly says. "Don't be a Jase and mind-fuck this for years before you realize love is love, either broke or having enough money to pay your kid's way through college."

And their kids, I think.

"Money doesn't mean anything to me. And—"

"It helps," Dad says.

"Dad," I huff.

"I'm glad I knew what it was like to go without it; makes you appreciate it more." He looks away from me and at Tags. "My family has money. It came from a loss. We were blessed. This may be a blessing. You may want to think about that."

Tags moves out of the booth. "Could you excuse me for a minute?"

Me? Oh God. I close my eyes and sit back.

"Bella."

I open my eyes and see his outstretched hand.

"Come on."

I slide out of the booth and take his hand, feeling relieved. But when we walk outside and he finally turns to face me, he doesn't look happy.

"Money doesn't mean anything to me."

"But he's right," he says.

"Is that why you brought us out here?" I ask. "Because—"

"No. You and I need to make decisions together. And ones without flashbacks of Little Bell's life, but what she sees as her tomorrows."

I'm confused.

He steps forward and grabs my face. "Is this your dream?"

"Yeah, but—"

"Is Mara gonna be an issue for my dream coming true?"

"Your dream?"

"Happiness, sweets. All-embracing happiness. Mara isn't coming after Luna, and David isn't pushing it. And you love me. You. You're my dream." He presses his forehead against mine, hands still on my face. "I'm so fucking in love with you, Isabella Steel. I don't want shit to come between—"

I reach up and grab the top of his hair, pulling his mouth down against mine. Lips, tongues, teeth, hands ... souls.

When my lips start to hurt and I need to breathe, I pull back. "I'm your dream?"

"Yeah." He laughs like he's confused. "Yeah, you are."

"Why is that funny?" I laugh.

"Because Sisco is going to have a field day with this."

"The guy from the studio in New York?"

"Our first date?" He smirks, and I laugh. "That'll be our story, okay?"

Our story, I sigh to myself.

"So, what do you say, sweets? Do we choose to become a happy, mundane couple? I'll work in New York, you'll work for your dad, and we'll see each other when we can. Or, do we take this opportunity and travel for the next five to eight months, fuck in ten different cities, and help make some other's dreams come true while we're living ours?"

"Hmm ..." I pretend to consider the choices. "I'll take fucking you in ten different cities, final answer."

He picks me up, twirls me around, and then sets me on my feet and gives me another breath-stealing kiss.

TWENTY-FOUR
TO THE MOON
TAGS

Standing outside the studio, my first day back, waiting to share the news with Sisco, I take a picture of the exact spot I saw Bella for the first time, that moment she turned around and I knew she was going to be mine. Then I send it to her.

She sends me back a picture of her tits.

"Well, fuck." I laugh as I zoom in on her nipples.

Then a text pops up.

Bella: *They miss you. ~ B.S.*

Laughing, I send a reply.

Me: *Wonder if I have flood insurance on my phone. Thing's soaked. ~ Tags*

Bella: *Now you know how my panties feel every time I look at you. ~ B.S.*

Me: *Miss you, sweets. Love you and your nips. ~ Tags*

Bella: *Have fun with Little Luna. ~ B.S.*

Me: *T minus three hours and counting. ~ Tags*

"They kick you out already?" Sisco laughs and gives me a bear hug.

"Actually, I got kicked up to producer." I step back. "How's business?"

"You don't get to ask how business is until you explain how the fuck you got a promotion. And it better not start with *I got fucked up and banged the wife I was trying to divorce*," he says as he unlocks the door.

"Actually, you remember the chick from my last night here?"

"Who could forget that?" He laughs and locks the door behind me.

"She showed up in Miami."

"Another Beverly wanting to sweep you off your feet?"

"No, she was hired as a producer. Shocked the shit out of me, but in a good way."

He looks up from his appointment book. "Yeah?"

"She's it, Sisco. She's the real fucking deal."

"So, you work together with this Beverly, your wife, and her father? How's that going?"

I explain pretty much the whole story in about two minutes, and when I mention Jase Steel, he laughs.

"Italian from Jersey?"

I nod.

He turns and pulls up the back of his shirt. "Gave me my first professional piece. Good man. He's her father?"

"Yeah, and I'm not sure he likes me."

"Tell him you love the Yankees, and he and his brothers will talk baseball with you for hours. So, Steel's girl, huh?" He laughs.

"My girl now." I sit down and lean back. "Unreal."

"You got your ass kicked for years; don't overthink it. Just enjoy."

"I plan to, Sisco. I plan to."

* * *

COMING HOME on a Monday was hell. She didn't want to go to school, but I could tell it was helping her grow. Was also kicking her ass.

She was exhausted. She fell asleep clinging to me, and I sat there holding her for a couple hours while Paula grilled me about Bella. Day one, and she's already asking when she and Luna get to meet her.

My morning and evening calls are with Bella. My every thought is Bella.

I try to figure out how soon is too quick for them to meet, but honestly, if we weren't taking over the show, I'd already have introduced them. But I don't want Luna to get attached and be missing her and me both.

Day two, and Luna has a full-blown breakdown, saying she doesn't want to go to school and manages to get so worked up that she vomits all down the front of me.

Two hours later, and she's passed out with a fever.

Lying in bed with her, my phone rings.

I look at the screen and hit *accept*. Or, at least I meant to.

Fumbling with my phone, I hit FaceTime on accident, and she answers too quickly to right my wrong.

She smiles. "Hey."

"Didn't mean to hit you up on FaceTime, but I'm working with one arm here."

"Tell me where that other hand is, and I'll join you."

I pull the phone farther away so she can get the full view. "Not so sexy, huh?"

"Oh my God!" She smiles. "Did you hear that?"

"Hear what?"

"My ovaries just exploded. I don't think I could handle seeing you two in person like that." She bites her bottom lip. "Damn."

"You know what's worse than exploding ovaries, sweets?"

"What?" She lies back on a plush, pale pink blanket

"Popping wood while your kid's laying on you because you are looking at the most beautiful chick on the planet, knowing what she tastes like."

"Carly warned me this would happen." She shakes her head.

"And what's that?"

"That I was gonna fall in love with her the moment I saw her. She said she already has." She rolls over onto her stomach and continues, "She also told me Dad mind-fucked her and my first meeting, and he almost blew it. So, while you're lying there like that, all I am thinking is when can I meet her and hoping you don't screw it up."

"I don't screw shit up. And you should've been here a couple hours ago when she threw a fit the size of Texas because she didn't want to go to school then threw up all down the front of me, Bella. Now that was hot."

"I'm ignoring that and just gonna put it out there that Dad and Carly rented a plantation in Richmond for two weeks. There's a pool, a pond, and some cute little places to visit. Join us."

"She's got school."

"She's three, Tags. She can miss a couple weeks."

"She needs it, Bella. She's got some issues that are best dealt with early on so she doesn't struggle later."

"Daddy." Luna sits up and looks at me. "I'm gonna get sick."

Sitting up, I put her head against my chest and mouth, "*Gotta go.*"

She nods and whispers, "Feel better, beautiful girl."

I wink at her then end the call, drop the phone, and grab the bowl on the floor next to the bed.

Day two of the fever, and I took her to the pediatrician. My moon has strep throat. She's on her first antibiotic and now is sound asleep.

Walking out of the bedroom, I see Paula looking over a pile of bills at the table. I smile to myself, knowing there isn't going to be a struggle this month or the next two. Plus, there's an added cushion for all the shit she doesn't do for herself often, because even without us here, things are tight for her. I don't know how she did it for the year I was gone, but she did.

I kiss the top of her head then walk over to get a cup of coffee. "You ever consider getting one of those one-cup machines, Paula?"

"I've had that Mr. Coffee longer than you've been alive. Still works. Why would I do that?"

I chuckle as I pour myself a cup. "Just wondering what Paula would do if she had a grand or two to blow?" I grab her cup then fill it up and set it in front of her as I sit down.

"Take a vacation. Haven't been out of this city in about twelve years."

"Where would you go?"

"I'd ask the cards."

I smile. "You'd ask your cards where you should go on vacation?"

"Then the tea leaves. And by then, I'd talk myself out of it ever being worth the trouble."

"Hi," I hear Luna's sleepy voice from the bedroom.

"Hey, sweet girl. I'm sorry I woke you."

Bella.

Shit.

"I got scratch throat."

"Ooo ... That's rough, huh?"

"I'll be okay. Who are you?"

Nearly sliding past the doorway, I grab the doorframe and manage to bust my ass on the wood floor.

"Daddy, are you okay?" She jumps off the bed, and then I hear her little feet coming closer. All I can do is fucking laugh.

Paula is laughing, I'm laughing, and Luna is wide-eyed and worried.

"I'm good, little moon. Just took a spill; that's all."

"You need the doctor? Maybe you got scratch throat?" She squats down beside me and feels my forehead. "And chills. I think you have chills."

"Little moon, you gonna be a doctor when you get older?" I pull her onto my belly and tickle her.

She laughs.

"You feel better now?"

"The robots made me better, I think."

"The what?" I sit up.

"Antibiotics?" comes from the bedroom.

Paula hauls ass past Luna and me and grabs the phone off the bed. "You must be Isabella."

Bella laughs. "And you're Paula."

"Where are you with all those trees around you?" she asks.

"Richmond, Virginia, ma'am. Family vacation and the next city of the show's stop."

Paula looks at me. "You know how you just asked me where I'd go, son?"

I nod.

"I'd go to where those trees are."

"Then pack a bag and get here. There's plenty of room." Bella laughs.

"She being serious, son?"

"He already shot me down," Bella states. "But you are more than welcome."

"And me?" Luna asks.

Bella beams. "You the most."

TWENTY-FIVE
RICHMOND
BELLA

At the airport, I'm pacing. I can't stop pacing.

"Would you relax already? She's three." Kiki laughs. "She's gonna like you, and if not, she'll love me."

I scowl at her, but she's not wrong. Kiki is the baby whisperer.

"She's gonna love you, too." I smile. "But still me more."

When I see yet another group of passengers coming, I hold my breath, and then I see him, with a tiny, little body wrapped around him.

"Jesus Christ, Bella."

"I know." I grin.

"You know you have daddy issues?" she asks, serious as can be.

I elbow her. "He's nothing like Dad."

"No, maybe not. But all the ladies are gonna look at him like they do Dad and the uncles. Can you handle that?"

"As long as it's me he's looking back at, it'll be just fine."

He pushes his shades up onto his head and gives me a millisecond wink.

"Well, that'll do it." Kiki sighs.

"You get your own man," I say as I watch him watching me.

"Oh, I plan to."

I whip around and look at her.

She rolls her eyes. "When I'm old enough, of course."

They're inside the tube, so I watch for the door to open, allowing them out. When they come out, I hear her crying and feel my heart crack a bit.

I hurry toward them. Then, unsure of what to do, I stop a foot from him. "Is she okay?"

"She can't hear herself talk." He steps forward. "Her ears. She'll be fine."

As he leans in to kiss my forehead, she cries out, "I will not!"

"Can I please have her?"

He arches an eyebrow. "That's how this is gonna be?"

"It will be when she's awake. And I'll do you a solid and teach her the joys of sleeping with earplugs in a house full of testosterone. I'm Kiki."

He smiles at her as I peel Luna off him. "Nice to meet you."

When he gives her a hug, she wiggles her eyebrows at me. I roll my eyes and ignore her.

"Luna, I'm Bella, and I have the coolest trick to teach you. I know you like dogs, but how do you feel about monkeys?"

I turn her around in my arms, and she yells, "I can't hear you!"

I smile and find the nearest bench, sit down, and she straddles me. "Plug your nose like this."

She does.

"Close your mouth and blow like this." I demonstrate but cross my eyes as I do it.

She looks at me like I'm nuts.

"Please?"

She does it then gasps.

"Did you hear a pop?"

She nods.

"Can you hear me better?"

She smiles and nods.

"You had to get the flight dust out of your ears. It happens every time. But now you know the trick."

"Thank ..." She pauses when she realizes she's still yelling and giggles. Then she hugs me. "Thank you."

"And thank you. It's been a long time since I've been able to share that secret with someone."

She sits back on my lap and looks me over, smiling a beautiful, little smile. "You're Daddy's friend."

"And yours, I hope."

She puts her hands on my cheeks. "And Paula's?"

"Of course."

"You're pretty, just like Princess Bell."

"You're beautiful, just like all the princesses, too."

"Is Daddy your Beast?"

I look up and see him looking down at me, bulging arms crossed over his broad chest. Then I look back at Luna, "Can I share another secret?"

She grins and leans in.

"I sure hope so."

She hugs me again.

When I stand up, Luna wraps herself around me Koala-style, and it's then I see Paula looking me over. I smile and mouth, "*Hi.*"

She nods then looks at Tags, pats his back, and then walks toward the luggage carousel.

Walking out of the airport with Luna on my hip, I watch as she takes in the sight.

Tags has already told me that she's never left the city, never slept anywhere but at Paula's place, and he wasn't sure how she would react. He also explained the issues she has faced. And even though I understand Mara a little more, I silently cry for the things Luna has endured, while my heart also breaks for Mara. When all the mayhem in her head is quelled, she isn't that bad. And as much as I hope someday Luna calls me Mom, I hope she can look at the woman who gave birth to her with love.

It took me a couple days to crush the little green beast inside of me that wanted the world to be flat for just a moment so I could push her off the side and into the unknown abyss. But when I allowed myself to take in his words and feel his love for me, it wasn't hard to see that my big badass has a heart just as big as his pierced dick.

Both of which I love about him.

"What do you think of Virginia?" I ask her.

"Richmond?" she asks, and I nod. "There isn't lots of people."

I laugh. "Much quieter than New York City."

She looks around in wonder. "Lots of green."

"Do you like green?"

"Do you?" she asks.

"I think it's beautiful."

She nods. "Me, too."

When Dad pulls up to the curb and the lift gate of the Denali is opened, Tags puts their bags inside.

Dad walks around the SUV, looks at Luna, and holds out his arms. "Come here for a second."

She looks at me.

"Luna, this is my dad, Jase. He's cool most of the time."

"She knows that, don't you, girl?"

Luna laughs as I hand her to him.

"How much do you weigh?"

Paula laughs. "I hope he doesn't ask all his passengers that question."

Dad holds out his hand and smiles. "Nice to meet you, Paula. I'm Jase."

She looks at his hand then up at him. "You the man who popped my boy in the nose?"

"Paula ..." Tags laughs.

"I got his back. As long as you're chill, I'm chill."

Dad smiles and nods. "Glad you do." Then he winks at her. "We chill?"

"And ... she's a goner," Kiki whispers then adds, "And to think I go to school with a bunch of nuns. His affect blocked by their love of Jesus."

"Okay, I'm thinking you're still too small for a booster seat, so we're going with the best seat in our ride." He opens the door. "Check that out, Luna. That's yours."

"What is it?"

"We always call our rides a she. This one's badass. Comes with a five-point harness and cup holders. Two in case you have a drink and a snack." He sets her in. "Safest one on the market, little moon. You know why?"

She laughs as she looks at it.

"Built of steel, safety guaranteed, and a ride you'll never forget."

"He never shuts it off, does he?" Kiki whispers.

"No." I laugh. "Never."

"How's that feel?" he asks Luna.

"Good."

"Tug at the straps to see if it's a good fit."

She tugs at them and nods.

"Okay, perfect. Should we take them with us?" He tosses his thumb over his shoulder at us.

She smiles and nods.

"You sure?"

She giggles. "Yes."

"Positive?"

"Uh-huh."

When he steps back, she's beaming.

He looks at Kiki. "And where do you think you got it from?"

"Mom, definitely Mom." Kiki laughs as she climbs in. "Hey, Luna, I'm Kiki."

She looks her over and waves.

"This may be a little overwhelming—meeting all these new people—but that also makes it super cool. Lots of new friends and fun times to be had."

"Do you have a dog?"

"No, my dad never loved me enough to get me one." Kiki pouts.

"Who's your dad?" Luna asks.

Dad laughs. "Not fair, Katherine. Not fair at all."

* * *

I SEE the door crack open and light peeks through the door. "She's asleep, Bella."

"What if she wakes up?"

"You drew her a map of the place, your dad has a video monitor in here. I'm sure there's an infrared alarm across the floor that will alert the state police the minute her toes touch the ground."

"Not the police, but I'll know," I hear Dad say from the other room.

"And he has the handheld receiver."

Dad laughs. "You have one, too."

"Leave them alone, Jase." Carly chuckles.

"But she's so snuggly," I whisper.

"That she is," he replies.

I give her a kiss on the back of the head then roll off my back and scoot off the bed. When I get to the door, I look back.

"She's whipped, sweets. Your crew has run her ragged, and I'm pretty sure she had the best day of her life."

I look up at him. "And this makes you sad, why?"

"Not sad." He gives me a quick peck. "Just eye-opening."

"In a good way or bad?"

"In a good way, but five to eight months too soon, if you know what I mean."

I follow him out to the living room.

"You should take her with you," Kiki says before popping a grape in her mouth.

"Yeah right." I laugh.

"Why not? Paula just said this is the first time she's flown, and now that she's done it, she wouldn't mind visiting her family in Germany." Kiki looks at her. "Cousins, right?"

"When the time is right," Paula says as she lifts a cup of coffee to her lips.

"The time is this summer. I have no desire to be slave to Steel's mail room. Take me with. I can hang out with Luna when you two are getting busy. I mean, when you two are busy."

Paula and Carly laugh. Dad? Not so much.

"Mail room summers help save for cars."

"So does Momma Joe," Kiki counters.

"Hard work is the foundation for you to build a stronger future on, Katherine."

"So is a trust fund, Dad."

He leans in, face all hard and intense. "The foundation comes from inside. You could inherit a million dollars, and if you don't understand how hard it was for those to make that possible for you, you'll lose it, Katherine. Then your kids, and their kids, and those in generations to come will be left not knowing how hard it is to come by and will end up with shit. Money is a huge responsibility, no matter how little or how much you have. Basics, Kiki. Basics."

"Well, I get loyalty, which to me would make me think of all those things for my kids, their kids, and generations to come. So you did good, Dad. Pat yourself on the back and let me do something for Paula, Bella, Tags, and Luna."

"It's cool, Kiki—Luna needs structure—but thanks for the offer." Tags sits down and pats the spot beside him.

"I already miss my boy; couldn't imagine not waking up to that little girl's face every day." Paula laughs.

Tags smiles. "And Paula can travel the world soon."

"You gonna make that happen, Tags?" Dad asks.

"With everything in my power."

Dad stands up. "You got a minute?"

"Oh, for the love of God, it's nine at night, Jase; leave the poor guy alone," Carly says, handing me a glass of wine.

Tags stands. "Sure."

TWENTY-SIX
THE PAST
TAGS

I sit across from Jase on the poolside wicker patio furniture and lean back.

"Bella's got some ideas."

I nod.

"I think they're great. I know this is what she wants, and I'd like to know what it is that you, Carter Taggert, want in life."

"I got what I want now."

"And what's that?" he asks, sitting back.

"The means to repay a woman who took in a teenager who didn't deserve it and an infant, a happy little girl, and a woman who I can see has the same bones and spirit I do. The rest will fall in line."

I brace myself for the shit he's about to spew, the shit I will take for her.

He sits back and nods.

"That's it?" I ask. "No right hook? No I don't deserve her? No my dick is bigger than yours?"

"We were good until the dick part, man." Jase takes a drink.

"Well, it is part of not only my anatomy but life." I sit back.

"Why don't you drink?"

"Never made a good decision while drinking."

He narrows his eyes slightly. "You smoke?"

"Cigarettes."

"Drugs?"

"You want me to piss in a cup?"

He laughs, and so do I.

"She know everything about you she needs to?" he asks.

"By you asking the question, I'm going to assume you've looked into me. And there's something in my past that doesn't mean shit to me, so no."

"You have a trust fund."

"Left by a woman who wanted nothing to do with me or my kid because I marked up her ex-husband's house when he left her and started a new family."

"The woman, your mother. Her ex, your father."

I shrug. "Something like that."

"They know Luna?"

"She had the chance, denied us both, then died. He doesn't get the chance."

"So, you know you have money, like a substantial amount, and you would rather struggle?"

"I'm aware, but you're wrong. This isn't a struggle; this is life, and it's pretty fucking sweet. Can't get my hands on it until I'm twenty-five, and when I can, it'll be for Luna."

"So, what would you say if I told you that David contacted me before we left and asked me if I was interested in buying the rights to the whole show?"

"I would say I would have a team of lawyers lock that shit over before signing a damn thing and only because you're Bella's father. Then I would tell you that you should ask Bella if she wants that kind of pressure."

"What if I told you I had no desire to oversee a project of this type and would have told him to stick it in his ass if I didn't think the two of you could make a shit ton of money doing what you love."

"I would—"

"And that my brothers and I would love to be guest judges from time to time?"

"I would say that would be up to you as the financier of the project."

"What if I said to you, I would finance it if you promised that, on your twenty-fifth birthday, you paid me back in full, that it was yours?"

I shake my head. "I don't want that money."

From behind me, I hear, "As one half of a couple, I'd ask that you consult your other half about that opportunity, if I were you."

Jase looks up, startled, and then shakes his head.

Clearly, this was no setup.

"And I'd tell my dad that I want half the financial responsibility, and I'm pissed that he didn't come to me with this first."

"I'd tell you that I wouldn't want to disrupt your flow. You have some killer ideas, kid. I hate TV and would watch your show. And those ideas are all you, which is why I've been telling you to save your ideas for when it's yours, not when you're still standing downstream of a good idea with piss-poor execution." He stands up. "And I leave you two with another decision." He kisses her head then pats my shoulder as he walks by. Then he stops.

"Tags, I like you, but what solidifies this brewing bromance is the fact that I really like your kid."

I can't help laughing at the irony. "Ditto."

As soon as he's out of sight, she drops onto my lap and wraps her arms around my neck. "My Brooklyn boy has bank."

"My Jersey girl seems to as well."

She leans in. "I would have totally judged you if I knew. Normally, people with money haven't a clue. They don't know the struggle."

"And you do?"

"You mocking or asking?"

"If we met here, not at the studio or in Miami, before I knew you, I totally would have still fucked you, but in a mocking way."

She laughs. "And how does one fuck in a mocking way?"

I shake my head.

"Spill it." She reaches down and grabs my dick.

"Can't mock-fuck you, Bella. You couldn't even play the role that you were born to if you wanted."

She squeezes now. "And what does that mean?"

"You could walk around with your nose up, acting like your shit smells like roses."

"Hold up. My shit, when I do shit, does in fact smell like roses. Got it?"

"Yeah, sweets, I do."

"Go on." Now she's rubbing up and down my shaft.

"You wouldn't lie there and beg to get off; you're an active"—I run my hand up her leg, up her tight, little belly, and under her sundress—"participant."

"Tell me more." She licks her lips.

"You got all the cute, little shit girls with money do—the silky hair, the clothes, the painted toes, the perfect panties, the waxed pussy—but you don't just lie there and expect to be pleased. You fuck, you suck, you get messy, and your fucking mouth is a dream."

"You like my mouth?"

"Every word, filthy or otherwise, that comes out of it." Lips against hers, I whisper, "Now turn that ass around, straddle me, and let me fuck you right here, right now."

"Yeah?" she asks, turning her body.

I reach down and pop the buttons, pull my cock out, push her panties aside, and push into her. "Nice and slow, sweets," I moan as she rocks against me. "Christ, I've missed you."

FOUR DAYS LATER, I'm sitting outside a southern plantation, looking over sprawling lawns, as Luna floats around the pool, not willing to let go of Kiki or Max, Bella's brother, the kid who spends eighty percent of his time in his room or the shower, nineteen percent eating, and one percent actually conversing with the family. The twenty percent he's with everyone, his nose is in his phone. I'm going to safely assume the other eighty percent he's on it as well, looking at shit no one wants to know about, with a table full of lawyers, Jase and smoking cigars. And yeah, Bella's smoking one, too.

We're celebrating our new baby, Moonlit Productions, owners Isabella Steel and Carter Taggart. We've acquired the creative rights to *Fifty Shades of Ink* and renamed it, *Convicted Ink*, which trademarked application is in process, so we own that together as well. We have a home base and are already working on an editing team. Now we're shopping designs, and Bella is impatiently waiting so she can start her marketing plan. Website, live feeds, social media for the show and the cast, and a million other things she's got firing off in her head.

The last signature needed is a contract naming Mara Gorgon as executive producer of this season's show. Totally Bella's idea. She wants her to have something for to work for, even though we've just signed our lives away and paid them off. Bella wants something for Mara to be proud of, something to tell Luna someday.

In the past five weeks, I have realized a few things about the world:

You don't like your path, change it.

When someone offers a hand, take it.

Real respect is earned.

True loyalty is a rarity.

And a steel heart is one you could love without worry and trust to love you back forever.

TWENTY-SEVEN
CONVICTED
BELLA

"Ten men, ten attitudes."

"Ten artists, ten cities."

"One will walk away with one hundred thousand dollars to start a new life."

"This is Convicted Ink."

"We're so badass." I lean against him as we watch ourselves introduce the show.

Tags chuckles. "You look sexy as fuck. I look like a fucking tool."

I pause the video, grab his face, and make him look at me. "Tell me I'm sexy, and I'm tell you you're sexier." I lean in and act like I'm going to kiss him then palm his face and push him back. "Until you admit we're sexy and badass, there's no kissing."

I hit *play* and hear a deep rumble from his chest.

"Not funny."

"What's funny is you can't tell me no. Never could."

Releasing my hand, he brushes his fingertips up my inner thigh.

I bat it away. "Luna and Kiki are sleeping right in the other room."

He leans in, completely ignoring me, moving fingertips from my inner thigh and up my sleep shorts, now nudging under my panties.

Leaning in, he whispers, "Kiss me."

"Nuh-uh." I lean back as he leans in and brushes his delicious full lips against mine.

"Kiss me, sweets."

"Nope," I whisper with absolutely zero conviction.

He traces his tongue over my lips, and I close my mouth.

"Killing me," he groans, rubbing a finger up and down my slit.

"Not fair."

He slides his tongue into my mouth as he slides his finger inside me.

I slide my tongue against his then wrap my lips around his tongue and suck it like I want to his beautiful cock, if I wasn't trying to prove a point ... and clearly failing, but I'm not really kissing him.

Leaning in more, he pushes against me until I'm on my back. Kissing me, fingering me, and pushing my shirt up, he palms my tit. Then he moves his lips to my cheek and whispers, "There is no sexier couple on this earth than us. But sweets, when I'm looking at your perfect tits"—he kisses one then the other then down my belly as he pulls my shorts down far enough to kiss my inner thigh—"when I'm seconds away from licking your pussy"—he pushes a second finger inside me—"there is nothing sexier. So, sweets, I look like a tool."

He stands up and loses his shirt. Then he bends down and picks me up so I'm eyeball-to-eyeball with him and says,

"You are sexy." He kisses my lips. "You are beautiful." He kisses me again. "And Isabella Steel"—he kicks our bedroom door shut, sets me on the floor, turns me around, pulls my shorts completely off, and he kisses my tattoo—"you are mine."

* * *

I WAKE up to the smell of coffee and bacon.

"Can she wake up yet, Daddy?"

"She's tired, baby girl."

"She didn't go to sleep with the moon?"

No, Luna, your daddy was a bad, bad boy last night, I think to myself.

"She woke up a few times, so she didn't sleep that well."

"I bet she did," Kiki says in her normal, snarky tone.

"Keeks, you wanna flip the eggs and shut your piehole?" Tags mutters.

"There's pieholes? Are they like donut holes?" Luna asks.

For a kid born with so many strikes against her, she is freaking amazing.

"You wanna pick up your pretties where you dropped them by the couch?"

I jump up, grab a tee-shirt, and throw it on. "Kiki, could you come in here please?"

"Momma Bell's awake." Kiki laughs. "Coming."

When she walks in, I shake my head. "You do know how much it took to convince him to pull Luna from school because you were more than capable of doing the same curriculum as she was doing?" I wrap my hair up in a messy bun. "That's not the education we were thinking."

"She's a smart girl; she's gonna pick up on clothes laying in the middle of the living room floor sooner or later."

"I was doing laundry."

"Yeah you were." She laughs and tosses my shorts at me.

I wad them up and throw them in her face.

"Luna, is that the alarm?"

"Time to call Paula!" she squeals. "Moon time?"

"Yeah, baby girl, different time zone. Time to send her the moon."

* * *

"THEY'RE HERE," Kiki says as the cars start to pull up to the plantation house we've been renting until we head to Flint, Michigan.

"I'll go greet them." Tags grabs the back of Kiki's shirt and pulls her back. "You stay here."

"Bully," she snaps.

He chuckles. "Remember that."

Looking out the window, I point them out as they exit the vehicles, "Maze, Grimm, Axel, Blade, Ranger, Darby, Breaker, Dagger, Neo, and Sisco. Sisco took Tags' place. He owns a shop in New York. He's doing him a favor by being here."

"All convicts?" Kiki asks, smiling.

"All have done their time."

"So, is it true what they say about bad boys?"

I hip-check her, and she almost falls over.

I laugh. "Girl, you aren't even ready for me."

When the guys come in, I have Luna on my hip.

Axel is the first one to hug me. "Guess no gummies for you this trip."

"Gummies?" Kiki asks.

"We tried to steal her stash." Axel smirks. "You must be J.B.?"

"Huh?" Kiki asks.

"Jail Bate," Maze clarifies from behind him.

"Where's the food?" Grimm asks.

"In the kitchen, scary guy." Luna points toward the kitchen.

"Thank you, Miss Luna."

Ranger walks in next. "Hey, boss lady." He hugs me. "Luna." He shakes her hand. "J.B." He lifts his chin.

"I hate your boyfriend," Kiki sneers.

While the guys eat the massive amounts of food that Tags, Luna, and Kiki made while I was editing, Tags explains the change in ownership and the direction of the show. We show them the footage from Vegas and reveal the name *Convicted Ink.* They all seem to like it, and even more than the name—the message behind it.

Second chances, new beginnings.

* * *

Tags
Crimson Door

"SWEETS." I hug her as she sobs against my chest. My heart literally aches for her. "It's all part of the show."

She shakes as she speaks, "He's so good."

"He lives in New York, right?"

"Probably in a box now."

There's a knock on the door to the office of Crimson Door Ink. "Give us a minute."

The door opens anyway, "Hey, man, if it's me, it's cool."

Bella looks back as she wipes her eyes. "Hey, Sisco."

"Not you, bro."

"Maze?" he asks.

I nod once.

"I'll take him."

"What?" Bella asks.

"Send me home this week. If he gets cut next week, which he will—"

"Sisco," Bella gasps.

"You have some really talented men out there. He's one of them. He won't last, though. Man's more interested in chatting with the clients than the art. He's good for a studio. People will love him, but for TV, he's not going to pull in the viewers."

"Man, you sure about this?"

He nods. "Already got it okayed with the judges."

Bella sniffs. "The judges are assholes."

"You do know they're your family, right?"

She nods and sniffs again. "Assholes."

Jase peeks his head in. "We good with Sisco?"

When he sees the look on her face, his eyes widen.

"Don't look at me like that!" she hisses.

"Little Bell, you need to toughen up."

TWENTY-EIGHT
TRAVEL TIME

TAGS

We've traveled to four cities this summer as Moonlit Productions. Flint, where Maze was cut, as expected; Portland, where Blade was sent home; and Austin, where Breaker was cut.

Bella keeps Mara in the know via email and occasional phone conversations. She's trying to make her feel like she's still a part of it. I know she's doing it to benefit Luna, but it shows just how big her heart is. And Mara, she's being decent to her, too.

The thing is, the Steel brothers know enough shops around that, so far, everyone had a studio waiting for them. I know damn well it was their way of stopping Bella from crying. And thank God for that, because it was hell.

Right now, we're on our way to New Jersey for ten days.

"She's exhausted." Bella kisses Luna's head as she lays across our laps; feet on me, head on Bella's.

Kiki smiles. "She's excited, though."

"I still think it's going to be a bit much for her." I rub her back. "Good, but a lot of change."

Bella smiles at me. "Paula will be there."

"I know, sweets, I know."

"And now that we're down to five and have rearranged the schedule, we'll be back every two weeks for two weeks."

"In a place of our own."

"Right down the road from Mamma Joe," Kiki adds.

Bella smiles. "God, I can't wait for you to meet her."

Kiki laughs. "I'm surprised she hasn't come home from Italy already."

"I bet she and Thomas are having the time of their lives."

"Yeah," Kiki says on a yawn.

"Go to sleep, Katherine Steel." Bella leans her head against her sister's. "You start school in just a few days."

"It's going to suck," she grumbles.

"If I made it, I know you can."

* * *

PULLING up in front of the townhouse that Bella and I are renting until we decide where and what we want to buy, I feel a sense of peace wash over me for the second time in the past four months.

"Sweets?"

She sits up and looks at me.

"I like it."

"Yeah?" She smiles.

"Yeah. And I know she will, too."

I turn and look at her. "You sure this will be enough? I've seen pictures of your childhood home."

"You gonna be here?"

I smile and nod.

"Luna, too?"

"Of course."

"Paula looking out for her when we're being badasses?'

I laugh.

"I'm going to be incredibly happy."

I kill the engine and look in the back seat to see Luna is sound asleep. "You think we can get her into the house without waking her up so we can Christian the entire place?"

She grins. "God, I hope so."

Bella unlocks the door after giving in to my request of allowing me to carry her across the threshold for the first time in our very first home, a tradition in the most untraditional manner. Then we head up the stairs, trying not to look around.

Inside the room with the yellow nightlight, Bella removes Luna's shoes, pulls back the blankets, and then I lay her in bed. We both give her goodnight kisses then very quietly back out of the room and shut the door.

I don't waste any time picking her up and kissing the hell out of her as I carry her down the stairs.

"Kitchen first?"

"Works for me," she says, grabbing the hem of her dress.

"Isabella?" an unknown voice comes from the kitchen, and I nearly drop her.

"Momma Joe?" Bella squeaks.

"So sorry to just barge in, but I saw you pull up."

Bella smiles, takes my hand, and then drags me and my hard-on behind her.

"Bella, you need to give me a minute," I whisper, but she doesn't seem to hear me.

"Momma Joe." She giggles as she lets go of my hand and runs into the kitchen, leaving me unshielded.

After they kiss and while they hug, Josephina looks over at me. When she laughs, all I can do is shrug.

"So, this must be Carter."

Bella turns and smiles at me. Then she sees the same damn thing her grandmother did.

"I'd offer you a piece of lasagna and garlic knots, but I have a feeling I'm interrupting."

"Um ..." Bella chews on her lip.

"I'd offer you a hug, but that may be more awkward than it already is."

"Oh my God, Tags." Bella palms her face.

I walk over and sit down at the large wooden kitchen table.

"So, yes to the lasagna?"

"I'd love a piece, Mrs. Steel."

"Joe is fine, son."

* * *

WE SPEND two weeks in our new community. Joe and her husband Thomas, Paula, Luna, Bella, and every other day or so, Jase, Carly, and the kids pop in. The community where we now live has a playground, an indoor and outdoor pool, gym, and so many other things and activities, like Friday night family movies that we've done as a family, a big, loud, eat way too many carbs kind of family.

We took Luna to her new school the first day, where all the parents were invited to stay, and we did ... the whole damn time.

Bella was amazing. She spent the entire day helping Luna make a list of her favorite things in her classroom.

Structure, she gets that Luna needs it, and I love her even more every day because, each day, another level of depth is revealed. And each night, I make sure I show her just how much she means to me.

Two weeks of setting up a new routine in a home with four bedrooms and an office that she spends way too many hours in when Luna is asleep, hell-bent on making every moment in Jersey special and burning the proverbial candle at each end, and now we have to say goodbye to my Luna ... our Luna, Paula, Jase, Carly, and Momma Joe, her siblings, but not the cousins who seem to really fucking hate me.

At the airport Bella squeezes my hand as we turn around and wave goodbye.

It was hell leaving Luna before, but I think it's even more so now that she's so fucking happy. I mean, she always has been, even going through all the shit she's been through. But this is a level of happiness that brings a tear to a grown man's eye.

We ended up sleeping the entire flight to San Fran, which was perfect because I was going to make damn sure we dated hard core while we weren't being Mom and Dad. We took a magic bus tour of the city and made out in the back of it like teenagers. We fucked at Billy Goat Hill on the tire swing. We went to shoot bows at the Golden Gate Archery Range, paddle-boating on Stow Lake, played put-put, went rock climbing, and Bella posted selfies of us every damn place we went. Oddly, her social media account is even bigger than the cast's. Apparently, happiness equates to more *hearts* than art.

We lose Darby but, as per the usual, he got a job in a week. Then we go home and do it all over again.

* * *

THE NEXT FEW months fly by. Home for two weeks, living some sort of normal, then to Honolulu. We have guest artists now, and all eliminations are done by online voting of our viewers.

We cliff-dived, swam with sea turtles and dolphin, went with the remaining guys to a few Hawaiian Luaus, and somehow ended getting dragged on stage and put in a grass skirts.

The last night we are there, we fly in a helicopter to the top of Diamond Head volcano.

Hovering over top, she holds my hand nervously.

Through my headset, I ask, "Would you jump with me if I asked you to?"

She laughs. "You're crazy!"

"Would you trust me, Isabella Steel, if I asked you to jump?"

"I guess so." She continues to laugh.

Taking a deep breath, I pull the ring out of my pocket. "What if I ask you to marry me? What would you say to that?"

Tears of a different variety well in her eyes as she opens and closes her mouth a few times.

"Isabella Steel, would you do me the honor of becoming my wife?"

She nods, leans over, and hugs me as she cries into my neck.

"I love you so much, Bella. So damn much."

After she calms down a bit, I tell her that I asked for her father, Carly, and Momma Joe's permission. Momma Joe insisted that her first granddaughter get her ring from when she married Jonathon Steel.

The next day was elimination day.

I keep Bella focused on planning a wedding. Every night, she spends an hour on the phone with Paula, Joe, her aunts, Kiki, Luna, and often times her female cousins, picking out everything for a New Year's Eve wedding.

* * *

KANSAS CITY, the date theme continues, and the crew is one less. Dagger went home.

Los Angeles at Halloween time, we have a blast doing every possible touristy thing there is to do.

When Axel gets sent home, Bella takes it hard. Truth be told, so do I. He's a great guy.

We were told we should stay in LA, enjoy it, but both Bella and I wanted to get home and walk the neighborhood with Luna. She is the moon, of course; Bella is the Sun; and somehow, I become a dog. I'm going to safely assume she was just reminding me of my promise.

Philadelphia was slotted as our last stop, but it's not anymore.

In Philly, we lose Grimm.

All that remains now is Neo and Ranger.

Our final show of the season is going to be live tomorrow and held in Jersey, in the studio called Forever Steel.

TWENTY-NINE
FOREVER STEEL
BELLA

At Tags' suggestion, we are doing our last show of the season live. He is as cool as a cucumber, and I'm the exact opposite.

When we arrive, the shop that always felt like home is packed with family and all of the cast that we began with. Dad and my uncles aren't going to be the only judges, so are all the members of the cast. And this week's theme is couples.

Ranger and Neo are both ready. They don't have a choice; we just told them the night before of our plans.

Tags decided we should dress up, making it a formal affair. Being a lover of fancy shoes, pretty dresses, and a hot, tattooed man in a suit, I was all for it.

When the cameras begin rolling, we stand, holding hands.

I begin, "We started with ten men, ten attitudes."

"Ten artists, ten cities," Tags continues.

"And tonight, one will walk away with one hundred thousand dollars to start a new life."

Tags nods. "This is ... *Convicted Ink*."

When the film begins, it shows all the men, tells the stories of their journeys, and where it has brought them. Tags holds me a little tighter when it's revealed that they all have jobs in studios that they love. Each man also taped a thank you to us, and that's when I really begin to tear up.

I look up at him when it's finished and smile. "Thank you so much."

"No, sweets, thank you for being mine."

Two couples are introduced—both of their stories were second chances—and then Neo and Ranger go to work.

Being live, as hosts, we have to keep the show going while they work, which normally isn't an issue, but I'm extra emotional.

"This week's about couples, so while the men work, how about you and I tell them our story, Bella?"

I laugh. "Why not? My family already knows."

"It started like this ..."

Again, a film starts, Tags' voice narrating it.

I look up at him. "When did you do all this?"

"I've had some extra time while you were on the phone, planning our wedding."

There are pictures of us with each of the guys, our dates, and lastly, a film of his proposal. This shocks me. Hell, he doesn't like being in front of the camera.

When it stops, he looks at me. "Hey, sweets?"

"Hey, Tags?"

"If I asked you to jump, would you?"

"Of course I would."

"And you trust me, right?"

"With my life."

"Do you know how excited I am to become your husband?"

"As excited as I am to become your wife."

He kisses me, and not a normal camera peck, but a fucking toe-curling, feel-it-between-my-legs kiss. And when he pulls back, he gives me a millisecond wink.

I feel a tug on my dress and look down.

Luna holds up her hand. "Come on."

"Where we going?" I ask.

"Take your time." Tags smiles sweetly.

* * *

Tags

I LOOK AT JASE, who smiles and gives me a nod then disappears down the hall. Then I look at the camera and say, "Just like the men you've met here on this show, I, too, have a past that includes a couple arrests. My creative outlet for all the knocks I took in life was always art. But on the streets and in the courts, they call it vandalism. With the help of a woman named Paula, I got my shit together. She told me to learn a trade, and I did.

"Sisco gave me a job in his shop. Under his guidance, I honed a skill, worked at it daily and legally"—I laugh, and so does everyone else in the studio, even the male cousins and Bella's brother who look at me like they want to kick my ass most of the time. A little freaky, but whatever—"and I became the best artist I could be.

"I saw a girl standing outside Sisco's studio back in May, the day before leaving to become a contestant on this show. It was lightning, and it was serene. Never felt that way before. Never will again. So, right now, as Neo and Ranger work on two couples who want their love to be forever etched on their bodies, the woman I love is in the back room of a studio where she grew up to know love, loyalty, art, and not to judge a book by its cover. She's back there with the people she loves the most, possibly in shock, because we were supposed to get married on New Year's Eve. When her father mentioned doing the final show here, I knew there was no other place that would mean as much to her as this one to start our lives together."

Axel laughs. "No shit?"

"None, brother."

"I'm hoping she can change quickly, or I'm going to have to stand here and talk a hell of a lot longer than I planned."

'Wild Love' by James Bay begins playing, and my racing heart slows.

Looking down the hallway, I see her cousin walking down the hall. Then I see Kiki with my moon.

She's doing really good, so fucking good. My chest tightens as I watch her dropping daisies with each step.

I look behind me and see Carly, Joe, and her aunts coming in the front door from the alley, as planned. Carly is smiling as tears fall down her face.

Jase

I FEEL my hands shake when she walks out of the bathroom. "You look beautiful, Little Bell."

"He loves me, Daddy, and I love him more than I ever thought possible."

"I know." I swallow hard as my eyes start to tear up.

"Please don't cry, Daddy. If you do, then I will, and ... Oh my God, I'm getting married today. I'm getting married here. Here, Dad." She hugs me so tightly that I'm sure she thinks I'm holding her together, but the reality is, she's doing that for me.

When she steps back, I hold her little face in my hands. "I love you so much, Bell, and I know that man out there does, too."

Her lip pouts out, just like it did … yesterday. It seems like yesterday.

I sniff and nod. "He does. The two of you are gonna have a beautiful life, so why don't we go make that happen now?"

She hugs me again, kisses my cheek, and then whispers, "I love you, Daddy."

Walking her down the hall, I focus on Carly. She's crying and smiling, and she's fucking beautiful.

He looks at my little girl just like I look at Carly. I knew it from the first time I saw him look at her. Pissed me off. Doesn't anymore.

I kiss my baby girl then give him a hug. "I'm trusting you with a big part of my heart."

"I'll guard it with my own. Thank you."

This is the time the audience will watch tape of all the art the two remaining contestants have created. Tags wanted it that way. He wanted their vows for him and her, for Luna, and for us.

With my arm around Carly, I hear the vows they exchange, traditional vows in a nontraditional setting with a very short ceremony.

When our priest pronounces them man and wife, Carly tightens her arms around my waist.

When he cups her beautiful face, he does it with reverence, just the way I want my little girl to feel for the rest of her life.

Carly whispers, "She did good, Jase."

When the kiss deepens, I'm a little hot around the collar. I mean, *what the fuck?*

Carly laughs, and I raise an eyebrow at her.

"Oh please, don't tell me you don't hope that part of her life is as good as ours."

"Baby, tell me you're joking."

"Not in the least."

"And Kiki, you want her—"

"Yep. And don't ask me about Max. You and I both know that boy is having sex at least ten times a day. It may be by himself, but—"

"Carly Steel, I'm gonna have to ask you to shut it down."

She pushes up on her toes and kisses me. Against my lips, she whispers, "I want you to rub that Steel ball all over my tongue."

"Who am I to deny the mother of the bride?" I give her a little Steel.

When Carly leans back and smiles up at me, I kiss her again. "Gotta close this thing down."

"I'll be here waiting."

"You better be."

I walk around the shop, or as the kids are now calling it, a studio and nod to the camera man focused on the men working on some pretty great tattoos.

"You ready?" The camera man mouths and I nod.

I move to the predetermined, spot, one that won't catch them on camera and begin.

"While our happy couple finishes up a kiss that's lasting a little longer than the father of the bride is comfortable with, let's check out the finished product."

The camera goes to Ranger, who's rinsing and wiping down the female's tattoo.

"Tell us about the piece."

"Tom and Pam wanted their pieces to represent him being her king and her being his queen. Instead of doing the typical card or going with a crown, gave them the idea to use both and add something a little personal. They're both of Irish descent, so Pam has the queen of clubs with a crown over one corner of it and his name above it. Tommy has the king of clubs, the crown, and Pam's name above it."

"Looks great, Ranger. How about you, Neo?"

"Ziggy and Slade wanted '*till death do we part*.' After a short conversation, I found out they met at Mardi Gras and both dig skulls. Slade has '*Till Death*' above his Mardi Gras inspired skull, and Ziggy has the words '*Do We Part*' over hers."

* * *

Bella

UNABLE TO FOCUS on anything but Tags, and he on me, Dad took over.

"We need to close this up." I smile at my husband.

He is mine.

"Viewer votes are sixty percent Ranger," Shelly, one of our interns, tells us.

I look at my uncles. "You guys have a favorite yet?"

"Always liked Ranger better, but Neo's work is better today. More detailed and more thoughtful."

I look at Tags. "I can't make the decision."

"Gotcha."

"So, who is it?"

"Gotta be Neo, Bella."

"But—"

He kisses me to crush my crazy. It happens every time I allow myself to get worked up.

"It's going to be fine."

I watch Tags stand in next to Dad.

"Today, we combined the scores of the in-studio judges and the online voters, and we have a winner. Today's winner gets one hundred thousand, and our runner-up will receive fifty thousand."

"With the judges scores and the viewer's votes, the winner of the fifty Gs is ... Ranger. That means Neo is *Convicted Ink's* season one's ultimate artist. Congratulations, man."

Champagne, confetti, and congratulations all around.

Neo, for the first time ever, looks at Tags with gratitude and not disdain.

"We have one more surprise." Tags smiles and holds his hand out to me.

"We do?"

"We do." He gives me a real wink, a husband wink, and whispers, "Go get Luna?"

Walking over with Luna, Tags smiles at her as he picks her up. "Are you happy, Luna?"

"The happiest. I have a mommy, Momma Bell."

"And I have a daughter who rules the moon."

She grins at me.

"I'm not gonna ever promise you anything I can't give you again, Luna." He looks past me. "Kiki, could you bring over the pup?"

Luna screeches, and I am pretty sure I do, too, as Kiki walks over with a tiny, little ball of black fur.

"Is it a boy or a girl, Daddy?"

"It's a girl."

"Her name is Midnight Moon."

"And just like that, Luna has named her new best friend." Kiki laughs.

"Is it a Bolognese?"

He nods.

"You're the best."

"No, sweet treat, we are."

EPILOGUE

Two steps, and her back is against the hotel room mattress, and I have my arm around her back, pulling her against me. I lift her chin with my other hand and crash my lips down on hers for a much-needed private kiss.

She immediately tangles her hands in my hair harshly and pulls me closer. She grips my lower lip between her teeth in a more aggressive move than she has ever made when my lips are on hers. Then she sucks hard, pulling at my lip, and I move in to grab hers. She then pushes her tongue into my mouth and licks so fucking deeply that I nearly lose it.

I reach lower with one hand and grab behind her knee, jacking it up around my hip while grinding against her. She moans when I pick her up and step forward, wanting her back against the wall to show her just how much I want her, just how fucking hard I am ... for her.

When she releases my hair and links her hands behind my neck, pulling herself up so her legs are around me, I groan

"Jesus Christ, sweets," I hiss as she crashes her mouth against mine ... again.

I pull back and set her down, "Gotta stop for a minute. Gotta show you something."

"Huh?" she asks confused as I step back further.

I pull my shirt over my head.

"You are the sexiest husband ever."

I turn so she can see my back. '*Forever Bella*'s' is written over my entire back now.

"Mine," she coos, "all mine." She reaches around me and grabs my dick.

"Easy, sweets." But then I decided I don't want it easy.

I turn, grab her up and pinning her against the wall, I grind against her as she sinks her teeth into my shoulder.

"Fuuuuck." I thrust against her, needing a connection. "My cock is so fucking hard for you, wife." I grind in as she licks up my neck.

With my head sticking out, begging for action, I unbutton my pants and immediately hit her bare skin.

"Bella, your pussy is so hot." I grind against her. "So fucking wet."

"I need you."

"When?" I start to slow down, a little tease to work her up even more.

"Now, dammit!" She buries her head in the crook of my neck as she reaches between us, grips my cock, and rubs it between her legs. "Oh God!" she cries as her head falls back and hits the wall.

I contemplate pulling out, making sure she's okay, but when she starts riding me, grinding against me, fucking ... me, I know damn well I'm not strong enough to deny myself or her.

"Fuck." I thrust in deeper, harder, faster.

Her moans, her cries, the sound of our flesh connecting, our bodies becoming slick with sweat as we fuck, it's like we have been apart for a lifetime.

"Fuck yes," I hiss as I pull her harder against me, turning us and walking quickly to the bed. I lay her down on top of the stark white duvet, grab her ankles, throw them up on my shoulders, and fuck her through our first orgasms. My cock is still not ready to stop, my body not ready to disconnect, and my fucking soul needs to show her who her soul belongs to.

"Your pussy is mine." I slam into her.

"Yes!" she cries.

I lean down and take her mouth, fucking it with my tongue, pushing hers aside. "Your mouth, mine!"

"Oh God," she sobs out.

I kiss and lick and scrape my teeth down her beautiful, long, slender neck. Then I take her nipple in my mouth and clamp down before sucking it out long and hard. I feel her body tense then shake as she grips the duvet and holds her breath.

I push myself back up and spread her legs open wide as I drive into her, watching my cock slide in and out of her. "Your cum"—I drive in harder, faster, deeper—"mine."

As she cries out, "Yes!" she comes so hard, so exquisitely.

I pull out and grip my cock, stroking it as I drop to my knees and lick her pussy until it's dry.

When she lies limply, panting, I stand up, still stroking myself. "Open your eyes, sweets. This is all yours."

She opens her beautiful blue, tear-stained eyes and watches as I jerk myself hard and fast before coming all over her belly. Then I flop down beside her, rest my head on her chest, and use my fingertips to rub my cum into her skin.

"No one else but me." She sniffs, her body shaking.

"No one else but you," I whisper before looking up at her. "No one ever again."

I hold my fingers up to her mouth. She wraps her hands around my wrists and sucks them clean.

"Fuck yes," I sigh.

After several minutes—hell, maybe hours of silence—I lift my head from her chest and look at her. "You wanna go again?"

"Husband, I could go forever. Forever Steel."

And I know she could.

"Forever mine. Forever Steel."

~ The End ~

NEXT IN STEEL

Ready for more next generation Steel?
Hell yes you are!
Eight more books will be released over the next several months, featuring the original Men of Steel.
WARNING!
This isn't their fathers story, it's all about the next generation of badass.
Preorder book one now!
Branded Steel

MEN OF STEEL
Branded Steel
Coming Soon

ALSO BY MJ FIELDS

THE STEEL WORLDS

(Recommended reading order)

The Men of Steel Series

Jase

Cyrus

Zandor

Xavier

Forever Family

Raising Steel

The Ties of Steel Series

Abe

Dominic

Eroe

Sabato

The Rockers of Steel Series

Memphis Black

Finn Beckett

River James

Billy Jeffers

The Match Duet

The Unsocial Dater

Match This!

ImPerfectly Matched!

The Steel Country Series

Hammered

Destroyed

Wasted

Tied in Steel series

Valentina

Paige

Gia

Steel Crew

(Generation 2)

Tagged Steel

Branded Steel (May 2021)

Title TBA (July 2020)

Title TBA (September 2020)

Title TBA (November 2020)

Title TBA (January 2021)

Title TBA (March 2021)

Title TBA (May 2021)

Title TBA (July 2021)

THE LEGACY SERIES FAMILY OF BOOKS

(Recommended reading order)

The Love Series

Blue Love

New Love

Sad Love

True Love

The Wrapped Series

Wrapped In Silk

Wrapped In Armor

Wrapped Always and Forever

The Burning Souls Series

Stained

Forged

Merged

LRAH Legacy Additions

Love You Anyway

Love Notes

The Way We Fell

The Truth About Love Series

27 Truths

27 Lies

The Firsts Series

Her First Kiss

His First Crush

Their First Fall

27 Truths About Their First Goodbye

Their First Time

The Norfolk Series

Irons

Shadows

Titan

Timeless Love series

Unraveled

Deserving Me

Hearts So Big

Couture Love

The Caldwell Brothers Series

(co-written w/ Chelsea Camaron)

Hendrix

Morrison

Jagger

Visibly Broken

Use Me

Standalones

Offensive Rebound

ABOUT THE AUTHOR

MJ Fields is a USA Today bestselling author of contemporary and new adult romance novels. She lives in New York with her daughter and smoochie faced Newfie, Theo.

When she's not locked away in the cave, she enjoys spending time with her family, listening to live music, watching theatre, singing off key, dancing to her own beat, listening to audio books, and reading— of course.

Forever Steel!

Join MJ's mailing list: http://bit.ly/MJFNews

Follow MJ on BookBub: bookbub.com/authors/mj-fields

ACKNOWLEDGMENTS

To all those who love the MEN OF STEEL,

You are the reason I get to do what I love everyday. You share your love of this world and that love, that loyalty to this family, is what this series has and will always be about.

Forever Steel!

To Andrew England,

You are the perfect Tags. Thank you for being the face of the first second generation Steel novel.

To Jules,

Thank you for you beautiful work with this series, love you.

To Autumn,

Thank you for being here and keeping me on task. It's never easy, lol.

To Kris,

This wouldn't have come together on time if not for

your help, and ability to work with me. A million thank yous.

To my reader group and ARC team,

I fucking love you all. #ForeverSteel style.

To Diane and Bobbie,

A special thank you for swooping in, last minute style, and helping polish and shine. Love you both so much.

To Kate Stewart,

You give good 'aftercare' girl. So glad to have you in my life, for the good times, and the bad.

To Chelsea Camaron,

This series kind of solidified our path, Forever Steel. Love you.

To Miss A,

When you're older we'll discuss the fact that my words may be disturbing to you now but someday babe, you'll get it...But not too soon okay?

The line "Don't ask me to stay when you taught me to fly"... That's for you to use in a couple years.

Love you... more.

Made in the USA
Columbia, SC
05 July 2024

38160806R00169